HANA-LANI

Other Novels by
Christine Sunderland

The Trilogy

Pilgrimage

Offerings

Inheritance

HANA-LANI

CHRISTINE SUNDERLAND

OAKTARA

WATERFORD, VIRGINIA

Hana-lani

Published in the U.S. by:
OakTara Publishers
P.O. Box 8, Waterford, VA 20197

Visit OakTara at **www.oaktara.com**

Cover design by Kay Chin Bishop, www.kaybishop.carbonmade.com
Cover image "Looking toward Kauiki Head, Hana," © 2010, Christine Sunderland
Author photo © 2007 by Brittany Sunderland

"Healing Prayer" from the *Episcopal Book of Common Prayer, 1928.*
Pele's quotation from Robert Wallace's *Hawaii* , Time-Life Books, 1977.
T.S. Eliot quotations from *Four Quartets*, Harcourt Brace, 1988.
Lindbergh's epitaph, taken directly from his gravestone, is Psalm 138:8, King James Version.
Quotation by Russell Kirk from Russell Kirk's *Eliot and His Age, T.S. Eliot's Moral Imagination in the Twentieth Century*, Random House, 1971.
Hymn, "O Worship the King," from *The Hymnal, 1940*, Church Hymnal Corporation, 288.

ISBN: 978-1-60290-260-2

Acknowledgments

I wish to acknowledge with gratitude:

Friends and family, who patiently read my many drafts and gave me invaluable suggestions.

Editors Margaret Lucke and Alfred J. Garrotto, who helped me develop and fine-tune *Hana-lani* into a compelling story.

Ramona Tucker and Jeff Nesbit of OakTara, who believed in my work and have walked me through the publishing process with their most excellent advice and encouragement.

The Hotel Hana-Maui, a peaceful and rural retreat set between the volcano Haleakala and the great pounding sea.

The open-hearted and gracious community of Hana. You have much to teach us; we have much to learn.

My dear husband, Harry, who introduced me to the incredibly beautiful culture and natural wonders of these Hawaiian islands.

Mahalo.

⌘⌘⌘

Duty is the conscience of love....
—WISE OLD WOMAN

Prologue

Old Nani-lei dusted the books lining the shelves as high as she could reach, singing to herself. The top rows were left to gather a thin white film rarely noticed in the room dimmed by draperies blocking the Hawaiian sun. Beyond the heavy panels, beyond the grassy bluff, even beyond the black cliffs, the sea crashed beneath the wide dome of sky, but Nani was content to keep the windows covered, for the books were precious to her grandson-in-law Henry, now in his middle age, and the sun was harsh. Some day she would open them for good, and the sea and the sky would flood the front room with their joy. But not yet.

No one in Hana town knew Nani's birth year exactly, and neither did Nani, nor did she care. She had seen generations come into this world and generations pass on to the better one, children grow to be adults, parents, grandparents. She had lived to 2004 much against her better judgment, but she was there for a reason, she knew, and she accepted this, not knowing what the reason was. Only last month Nani had buried her brother, over a hundred years on this good earth, and now she was the last of her generation. There had been nine of them, two older brothers and six younger sisters, and she had buried them all, the last being Willie. She buried many of the next generation too, a son and a daughter, nieces and nephews. Now Willie rested in the church graveyard with other Browns, Kaelanis, and Fitzhughs. He rested alongside her granddaughter Maria, drowned nearly two years ago.

Nani wore loose flowered cotton over her ample body, and her fleshy arms emerged from cap sleeves woven with ribbons. Her feet were bare most of the time, but for outdoors she liked her rubber sandals from Hasegawa's General Store. She moved slowly, gliding about the house, her wide hips swaying to music only she could hear, as she cared for Maria's husband, Henry, and his little Lucy, her fifth great-grandchild. She was mighty proud of it, too, proud to be a *tutu*, a grandmother of many.

She finished the shelves and tables in the living room, and moved to the banister that led to the upper bedrooms. She polished the wood with lemon oil, rubbing a thick cotton towel along its grain as her mother had taught. The wood gleamed, the grains both dark and light moving up and down, rather like people, she thought. She loved Hana-lani, the old house that was her birth-home, a clapboard assortment of rooms and extensions that had grown with her own years, and as she worked, she prayed, her cross and her medal of Saint Christopher, patron of sailors, damp against her heart. Sometimes the silver chains entwined, and she had to untangle them with her fingers.

Nani finished the banister and moved to the kitchen to check on Lucy, busy coloring at the table. The child's dark curls brushed the newsprint tablet as she bent close to her work, her tiny fingers grasping a red crayon. She looked up and grinned, and Nani could see with satisfaction two teeth breaking through the upper gum to replace those taken by the tooth fairy. The child, seeing her tutu pause, returned to the page to fill in the petals of a hibiscus flower. A sweet girl, Nani thought, but she should be in school. Nani adjusted Lucy's hearing aid, attached to a band worn over her head. The child had been born with the impediment, as they called it, but this little gadget helped. They were a good fit, Nani thought, the old grandmother and the grieving grandson-in-law and the partially deaf child. And Lucy had grown, fed by Nani's love and listening, from four to five to six and nearly seven now, running over the lawns that lapped the house, collecting yellow plumeria to string into fragrant leis, as the sea pounded the cliffs far below.

She checked her taro chunks boiling in a pot on the black iron stove and stabbed them with a fork. These should make enough *poi* for the rest of the week, and she would mash them to a fine pulp to work between her gums. She searched for her masher, looking through assorted appliances, gifts she refused to exchange, each one holding the heart of the giver. She would portion the poi into small plastic tubs with snap-on lids to freeze, as she did with her vegetable stew, pureed, so she would never go hungry. She loved the story of the Little Red Hen who worked so hard on that loaf of bread. She tried to do the same.

Tutu Nani found the masher and set it out, ready. She filled the kettle. Summertime she brewed pineapple tea on the stoop, but this was February and she preferred Noni tea, the herbal remedy against colds and flu. They did have winter in Maui, contrary to what some folks thought. Winter was the rainy season, and the temperatures dropped a bit too. She pulled a bamboo tray from a lower cupboard, set a mug on a cracked saucer, and waited for the water to heat. Henry wanted his tea in his study today, and she would oblige, in hopes he would forgo the rum. She often wondered what he wrote in the makeshift office, but she could not read and was content to help him however she could.

Nani poked the taro again and glanced through the kitchen window. The sun had disappeared suddenly, as it often did, and the afternoon sky was dark with black clouds pushed by the wind. Farther out, the sea churned, sending white caps in a mad dance over the surface. Nani knew of the sea and its lore, how outriggers with their boat gardens followed the stars to Hawaii, how they crossed the oceans from Tahiti so long ago, an ancient line of adventurers going back even to India. She knew the tales of Hana and the sugar fields, and the time when white cattle grazed on the grassy slopes of Haleakala. She recalled the building of Fagan's cross, planted high on the ridge under Pele's volcano, reflecting a new way of worship, a more peaceful way, she thought. She knew of the mountain's stormy past and quiet present, sure that both would form the future, and she sensed she bridged the mountain and the sea with her huge soul, a soul holding time before, time now, and time to come.

The kettle boiled and steamed, whistling its vapor into the still air. Nani poured the hot water over bark shavings in a clay pot, brewing the mulberry tea her family had made ever since she could remember, a family that carried the blood of many cultures in its veins. Indeed, she believed she was related to every soul in Hana—Samoans, Filipinos, Japanese, Chinese, Koreans, even the *haoles*—and her stories wove these threads together into a patchwork quilt she wore over her heart, warming the broken places.

Over the years she had waited tables and made beds. She taught music and dance to the *keikis* in school and played her ukulele in the

Congregational church, sitting cross-legged and humming, as her eyes roamed to the rose window over the front door and the people sang "Fairest Lord Jesus." At family gatherings, she danced the soft sway of the island hula to "Aloha Oe" and tried to move her hands like a ballerina, her mottled fingers painting the air with stories of love and war. Pieces of those years cluttered the rooms of the house, for she could not give things up easily—dried flowers in a school yearbook, photos of her children and their children, faded and smudged with fingerprints. Most dear were Lucy's pictures, swathes of vivid greens and pinks and deep sea-blues, tacked wherever a bit of blank wall could be found.

Nani poured the tea through a strainer into a mug, stirred in honey, and carried the tray to Henry's study. Lucy padded close behind. The old woman paused outside Henry's door, grief hitting her heart. She breathed deeply.

When Maria had drowned in the cold waters of San Francisco Bay, Henry left his teaching job at the university and came home to Hanalani with Lucy, as was right, for Nani had seen to his raising since he was twelve. Nani gave him the living room for his books and didn't mind the shelves that covered the walls and the draperies that covered the windows. Henry was happy to sleep on a cot in the adjoining den and Lucy slept in his old room, the sun porch in the back. He asked for quiet, for solitude. He seemed relieved when Nani took over the routine of living—the cooking, cleaning, mending, washing, and above all, the care of Lucy Maria.

The dark-haired child with the soulful eyes was a painful reminder, Nani saw, of his beloved Maria, and the grandmother prayed her grandson would be healed of the grief demons, for she saw him plunge farther and farther into the abyss. If he fell too far, she feared she could not reach him. So in her grief, she watched over them, weaving them together as best she could, allowing the spirits of past, present, and future to work through her, under the mountain on the edge of the sea, in the wild grass surrounded by the rich rain forest.

Lucy knocked on the door and reached to open it with her small brown hand.

One

San *Francisco* magazine said she was one of the most eligible women in town, and Meredith Campbell agreed. It was nice to be appreciated since moving from New York, nice to be admired in the party circuit. She had arrived at the City by the Bay in early 2002, so it had taken her only two years to get her name in print.

The workout room was packed with slim bodies, pushing and pulling, engaging steel levers and weights, grinding rubber soles onto moving belts. Above the whirring of the machines and the beeping digital read-outs, a rock band wailed as the February rain fell silently outside the double-paned windows of the tenth-floor club.

She flipped her cell shut, thought better of it, flipped it open, and tapped another number. She had finished twenty minutes on the Stairmaster and read her results: 178 calories. Not bad. Unlike some women who let themselves go, she worked hard, two hours daily, to meet her standards, but it seemed she could never *quite* meet them; she could never be *quite* like those models in the magazines. Still, her legs were long with muscular calves, her thighs toned, her tummy *almost* flat, her hips just wide enough to be alluring, her waist sweet and narrow. Her breasts tilted up nicely, impressive in her stretch camisole. She couldn't complain about her facial features, either, with the high cheekbones, wide-set blue eyes, star smile, and thick blond hair falling to her shoulders. She had come to expect men to melt at first glance.

Holding the phone to her ear, Meredith waited, counting the rings, not wanting to leave a message. "Pick up, Parker, pick up." She wiped her brow and climbed off the Stairmaster.

"Parker Kirby, Accounts," Parker said in her clipped voice, sounding rushed as usual.

"They fired me," Meredith hissed as she slipped her magazine, folded back on "How to Find Love," into her Gucci tote alongside the

Chronicle's horoscope page. The astrologer had predicted today would not be good.

"No! From your nice cushy job?"

"Yes, from my nice cushy job—the one you got for me, remember?" Meredith reached for her towel and headed for the locker room.

"The one Daddy got for you. You *do* interview well. Did he really fire you?"

Meredith's job had been good, really—six months of meeting and greeting clients, including her current roommate, Nick, but she *had* missed a few days.

"He may as well have, but no, it was that Mapleton lady, the old witch. She said my attire wasn't appropriate and my attendance irregular. I couldn't pass up that ski trip with Nick—I'd be a fool. And *my attire* is what everyone wears these days. She's a real Victorian, if you ask me."

"I told you your skirt was too short and your cami too tight. Too much leg and too much cleavage. You can't dress like that at the office of Kirby and Calhoun, not with your body." Parker laughed. "And I found the doc for that, don't forget."

"But *I* paid for it." It was worth every penny—the silicone enhancements, the nose job, and she was considering a tummy tuck, but maybe not right away, considering her bank balance. At thirty-six, she needn't worry about Botox. She moved her hand over her thigh, adjusted the black Lycra, and smiled at a well-built young man staring from the weight room.

"Parker, maybe you could talk to your father." Meredith paused and stretched out a sculpted hamstring.

"No can do, my beauty, no can do. Daddy left for London this morning."

⌘ ⌘ ⌘

Meredith climbed the stairs to her third floor apartment on Taylor, halfway between her Nob Hill sports club and the Union Square shops, a convenient location. Nick wouldn't be home for hours. She could enjoy a hot bath, maybe call her masseuse, and be ready with champagne, wearing the black negligee he bought her. Being unemployed did have its advantages. Bubbles and hot water were nearly as soothing as sex and kept the dragon at bay, that uneasy feeling she might topple into the void, into nothingness.

Had she always felt that emptiness? That dizzying fear of being on the edge of the world, alone? Did everyone feel it? Newness helped banish the fear, smother it. Shopping gave her a nice rush as she carried her bags through a boutique door, planning how the pieces would fit into her ever-changing wardrobe. New was good. New was fresh and raw and untouched. New had edge and the surprise of the unknown, the unexplored. But better than new was sex, and best of all was new sex. In the early stages of a relationship, sex satisfied that need for— how could she define it—something intimate yet infinite. But even with sex, she hadn't been able to retain the feeling for long. Nick had been the longest, nearly three months, but *he* was a doctor with good hands.

One more floor. She tightened and released her abdominals as she climbed. Fitness could fill the void, and the right body would surely help, as well as the right job and the right man. That man *could* be Nick. Nick was *so* right in *so* many ways. He was easy on the eyes for starters, and he had a significant income as a surgeon. It was merely a matter of watching her diet and working out, exploring all aspects of seduction and achievement. Multi-talented women possessed power. They owned their lives, controlled their world, fulfilled their dreams. She was nearly there, by anyone's standard, or had been, until this job thing. Well, it was their loss. Her expertise would save someone else's company. And in the meantime Nick would console her, help with the rent, and keep her dragons at bay.

Meredith opened the door and threw her jacket on the white leather couch. In the weak light dimmed by high-rises and dark skies, she again appreciated the clean lines and muted tones of the condo's decor—the chrome chairs, the cream walls, the vanilla carpet so thick under her feet. The new rug had been Nick's idea when he moved in, and she smiled as she recalled their first tumble to test it out. The plasma TV with surround sound was his contribution as well, covering most of one wall, and the screen greeted her like a friend, inviting her to pause, relax, unwind, absorb another's thoughts, experience another's feelings, a kind of vicarious pleasure and pain. They watched the news, and old movies too, or tried to, often finding the flashing images and voices arousing, like having sex in public.

She turned toward the long kitchen off the dining nook. The charcoal granite counter was bare except for a few artistically placed whisks, ladles, and spatulas in stainless steel holders. She checked on the goldfish a neighbor had left with her to feed. She frowned. The orange body floated on the water's surface, scales glistening.

Meredith ran her fingers along the smooth sides of the glass bowl as though she could bring the fish back to life. The boy in 2B had shoved it into her hands, and his mother had looked at her imploringly, offering a small canister of flakes. It was a moment of weakness, she thought now, as the floating fish accused her. She would find another one. Didn't they all look alike? The kid wouldn't know the difference.

She opened the refrigerator. Not much there. They rarely cooked, and Nick was as punctilious as she. No leftovers or old produce waited to be thrown out, no cheese molded in plastic drawers, and no eggs or butter or milk were getting past pull date. Several mineral waters, some vermouth, a lemon, and a jar of olives sat on the top shelf. Next to the olives was a bottle of champagne. At first relieved there was a chilled one waiting, she looked closer. Only half-full. She didn't recall opening it.

She reached for a mineral water and twisted the cap. As she put it to her lips, she heard someone laughing from down the hall. A woman. Nick's deep voice. What was going on?

She stepped slowly toward the bedroom. A pair of women's penny loafers lay on the carpet. Meredith stared at the shoes, then at the closed door.

She opened it slowly, her heart racing.

A woman's head slipped under the sheet. Nick looked up, raising himself on an elbow, his brown eyes wide with surprise, his face flushed, his thick hair sweaty.

"It's not what you think," he said as if reading lines.

4

"Yeah, sure." She grabbed his hospital ID and trousers and slammed the door behind her. Had she really seen that?

She gripped the pants in her fingers. She had never doubted Nick's adoration. After all, she had saved him from his boring marriage. What a fool she was, she thought as she tossed her neat bundle out the kitchen window into the back alley, where it landed squarely in the dumpster. *Yes.* A small satisfaction, but appropriate.

She found her jacket and tote, slammed the door, and walked down the stairs, numb. It wasn't until she reached the street that she realized the woman was *Ashley*, his *wife*. She was ten years older than Meredith, at least ten pounds heavier, and her hair was a mousy brown.

Meredith paused in front of her building and stared at the traffic. *How could he?* Her chest throbbed and her throat was dry. She swayed and sat on the porch steps. What had happened? She and Nick had been close. She was *sure* they had been close. She was *sure* he loved her. Even though they never said the words, she knew it. How could he do this? The bedroom scene flashed through her mind like TV news, again and again. There was Nick, replayed and replayed, his sweaty face so surprised.

She clutched her knees. Wasn't she good enough? And with his wife!

She shook her head, gripped her bag, and headed for Parker's office. Parker would know what to do. Meredith pulled out her cell and tapped her friend's number with the nail of her index finger.

"He was with Ashley," she said, raising her voice above the traffic. She cut through Union Square, passing a new café and street musicians. Nick with Ashley did not make a pretty picture. Maybe her therapist could exorcise it.

"That can't be." Parker sounded interested but distracted.

"Meet me somewhere, Parker. This is serious. I'm falling apart."

"I've got things going on here. Just a sec."

Meredith maneuvered through the crowds, past an animal rights demonstration at Neiman Marcus, and on toward Grant Avenue.

"Okay," Parker returned, sounding out of breath. "He's gone. Meet me at Buzz's. I want to hear all about it. Geez, Meredith, I'm so sorry."

Meredith flipped her phone shut and inhaled deeply, tightening her abs, working that tummy. By the time she approached the steel-and-glass skyscraper that leased the top floor to Buzz's Bar, she had resolved to get Nick back. He was so right for her; he didn't want children since he had three already, and she could *not* tolerate children.

Parker would have ideas how to remedy this temporary setback, and bring him to his senses. After all, Meredith was gorgeous. Everyone said so; they had always said so. She accepted her svelte curves and classic bone structure as her just due. This job thing and Nick's slight error in judgment were simply blips on the screen. She slipped through the revolving doors as the guards in the lobby stared. Men *do* like leather and tights, she thought, especially when a red camisole shows a little cleavage.

As she rode up the elevator, the image returned, Nick looking up at her, guilty. How could he? This was *not* a good day.

⌘ ⌘ ⌘

It was early to be at Buzz's, only four, but locals were beginning to arrive. They lingered around the chrome bar, dangled legs from retro stools, and partnered at Formica tables with potted ferns. A female vocalist wailed above the clatter of glasses and ice-crushing blenders.

"Play hard to get." Parker stirred a martini with her baby finger. She pulled out the olive and sucked on it. Her strawberry curls fell to her shoulders, and she raised a knowing brow over pink-shadowed lids that matched her lip-gloss. "That's what *I* usually do. Men generally want what they can't have. They're simple souls, really."

Meredith had never played hard to get. How many had there been? Did it matter? It was a liberating time to be alive, a time when a woman, just like a man, could have what she wanted or *who* she wanted, when she wanted. No commitment, no baby complications. Her morning-after pills had come in handy, and the one pregnancy she had blundered into had been neatly erased by Parker's sister, a fertility specialist. The stinging metal, the twinges of regret, and lingering guilt had been successfully buried, deep in her memory. Why should she even think about the abortion? After all, it was her choice, and the law of the land backed her up. If the law said it was okay, well then, *duh*.

"Hard to get?" Meredith motioned to the waiter for a martini like Parker's. "I don't think so."

"Yeah, like Scarlett and Rhett."

"In *Gone with the Wind?*"

"Yeah." Parker's eyes roamed.

"What if he doesn't fall for it? What if he believes I'm seriously leaving him?"

"No chance."

Meredith followed her friend's gaze to a cowboy at the far end of the room. He wore a three-piece suit and a broad-brimmed hat.

Parker whistled through her teeth. "Whoa baby, look at that guy. Matching pocket scarf."

"He's unavailable, remember? That's the newsman from the magazine show."

"You're right. I thought I recognized him. He's gay, another man lost to grazing women. This town gets worse every year. I don't know why I don't go to Texas or something, where there are real men. The number here is dwindling fast." She shook her head and sighed.

"Parker, you're not helping." Meredith slipped a strand of hair behind her ear and pulled her camisole down farther.

"Okay, go to Maui."

"Maui?"

"Go anywhere warm and tropical and romantic, so when Nick finds you, you're in the right place, tanned, wearing appropriate clothing, or not wearing, as the case may be." Parker waved her fingers through the air, her rings flashing, her bracelets jangling, as though she were pitching a Hollywood scene. "Remember the Bahamas, our junior year?" she said, giggling.

Meredith grinned. They had hooked up with two Yalies. It *had* been good. Was it Roy and Carter? No, it had to be Billy and Calum....

"Maybe you're right. I've got a little leeway on my plastic." Suddenly she regretted spending her paycheck as soon as she received it, sometimes sooner, and wished she had opened a savings account as her father had advised. But she had some room on her cards, and a few of them had never been used. It might be time to break them in.

"No maybes. Book the flight now." Parker eyed Meredith's cell in the side pocket of her bag.

"Maui? I haven't been to Maui since college." She had been careless on that trip, a lesson she wouldn't forget. He was a sweet boy, too, a local, with incredible biceps. They parasailed. He sucked her toes. They had sex on the beach.

"Stay at the Hotel Hana. I honeymooned there with number one."

"Number one? You mean Terry?"

"Yeah, Terry." Parker sighed, drifting away. "He had some bod, that Terry, and the place is a real sweet hideaway. I wonder what he's doing these days."

Meredith recalled the moist heat of the islands, the trade winds ruffling silk pareos, the aromas of jasmine and plumeria. She drank fruity rum cocktails with tiny parasols and wore clinging string bikinis. Her tan showed off her white teeth and blue eyes. She could use a little sun, aroma therapy, and yoga on a daily basis. Waiters would stare; porters would compete to carry her bags. Nick would be putty when he arrived.

"Tell me about it," Meredith said as she reached for her second martini.

"They say it's the top-rated getaway for the year. Posh. Very romantic. Private cabins and hot tubs. Crashing surf. Black sand beach. And it's at the foot of Haleakala."

"Haleakala?"

"The volcano."

"You're kidding."

"An inactive volcano, not to worry, but, like, it's different, right? Something new? Ever made love at the foot of a volcano?"

"Can't say I have."

"The hotel has a fabulous spa with all the latest treatments, a huge pool, even horses. Now that's sexy."

Meredith saw herself riding with Nick through frothy waves crashing on the beach. She straddled a palomino in high-cut shorts, galloping, up and down, up and down, her hair flying, the sea air fresh against her cheeks, Nick in pursuit. He would dismount, pull her off, and they would make love on the sand like Deborah Kerr and Burt

Lancaster in *From Here to Eternity*.

"I'll need a new wardrobe," Meredith said. She saw flowered bikinis and bronzed skin, wet and glistening, as she rose from the surf, like an updated Bo Derek in *Ten*.

"Then go shopping. Something new always lifts my spirits. Start over with everything."

"I'll do it." Meredith smiled as she recalled a sale at Saks. "I'll do it." She flipped open her cell and tapped a number with a crimson nail. "Thanks, Parker."

Two

Meredith slipped into the back seat of the taxi, cursing the torn vinyl. She set her large Kelly bag alongside and hoped her luggage wouldn't be soiled in the trunk.

"The airport, domestic terminal," she said.

The driver nodded and headed across town to the freeway, beating time on the steering wheel to blaring reggae. A photo of three children hung under his permit, and a plastic Virgin Mary dangled from the mirror.

Meredith had returned to her apartment to find Nick had moved out. Just like that! The note read, *Sorry, babe, it's over.* Surely, she thought, he would call. But he didn't. Nor did he return her calls. Undeterred, she shopped and packed and ordered the taxi. Plan B. Parker was right.

The driver turned onto Gough, and Meredith pulled out her phone. No message. She rescheduled her personal trainer, her masseuse, her therapist, her hairdresser. Should she let her mother know?

She thought not. Her mother wouldn't care where she was or what she was doing. Marketing for Chanel filled her life, along with her numerous girlfriends. Meredith winced as she recalled visiting her mother in Paris. It was fun, the men intriguing, the champagne and *foie gras* delicious. The eighth arrondissement flat placed them near the designer houses—Gucci, Christian Dior, Louis Feraud, Celine, Prada. Her mother got her into the shows, where the great shoppers of the world watched slinky models slide down the runway, turning on their heels, their eyes steely and cool. Meredith had practiced the look—raised brow, lowered lid, scowl—and found it effective.

But her mother grew impatient with her daughter staying on, and staying on, and finally kicked her out. There was no other way to say it. She kicked out Meredith, her only daughter.

As the driver took the on-ramp to 101 South, Meredith folded her phone and examined her nails, noting that the extra coat was holding up well. After Paris, she had come to San Francisco, thanks to Parker who was from SF and knew people, the right sort of people. Parker had welcomed her with open arms, as did many of Parker's male friends. San Francisco didn't have the pace of hometown New York, but it served nicely at this point in time.

She wouldn't call her mother in Paris. And her father was beyond caring. His heart attack *in the act*—appropriate, Meredith thought— had left wives one, two, and three, as well as Meredith, her brother, and scattered half-siblings, with only debts and his ghostly presence in a Florida rest home. But he had enjoyed life. She gave him credit for that. He worked hard on Wall Street, evaded the SEC sweeps, made a bundle, played hard, and spent the bundle and then some.

The taxi followed the freeway along the bay, past Candlestick Park, through South San Francisco, Brisbane.

Meredith had visited her father at Christmas. He lay in a gray-green room that smelled of urine. The tubes of life wound around him like snakes. His watery eyes darted about and briefly rested on her. She took his hand, and his fingers moved slightly. This was not the father she had known growing up, the man who taught her to ski, to play touch football, to follow the Yankees on the sports page. This was not the man who had taken his princess shopping at Bergdorf's and waited in Queen Anne chairs as she modeled a dress for Christmas, Easter, or the symphony. Could this man, lying so helpless and gray, be the father she had visited when she was ten, every other Saturday, climbing six floors to his brownstone flat, and later counted the days to the next visit, marking them off on her Barbie calendar?

He was not, could not, be the same man. In the sour green room, she had gazed at the creature in the tilted bed, and as his eyes held hers, full of hope and love, and possibly regret, her heart choked. She knew tears were coming. She kissed him lightly on his forehead and walked out. There was no point in wasting her time. Life was for the young. You had to look out for yourself in this world, *numero uno*, treat yourself right. Why, she recently read a magazine article on the virtues of "healthy selfishness," written by two psychologists. Her father would have agreed with them.

As the taxi headed down the off ramp Meredith wondered if her father's physical therapy was doing any good, and shoved the image of his broken body to the back of her mind. He may as well be dead, she thought. What kind of life did he have? She almost wished he would fade quietly away.

They pulled up to curbside check-in, and Meredith shivered. She sensed this trip would change her, and she had no desire to be changed. But she had come this far, with new matched luggage crammed with silk panties and bright bikinis. She buried her unease with images of giant Mai Tais and coral sunsets, paid the driver, and turned toward the porter.

"Kahului, Maui." She handed him the e-ticket as she set down her bags.

Her phone jangled. It was Parker, sounding amused. "I asked Daddy about the job."

"And?" Meredith tipped the attendant and stepped into the terminal, looking for a route through the crowds to the security checkpoint and gate.

"He was as surprised as you were. I think he liked your company uniform, but he can't upset Mapleton. He said she's the brains behind the business, and the partners would have his head. Sorry, did my best."

"That's okay, Parker. Thanks for trying. Gotta go. Heading for the gate."

"Sure. Aloha, kid. Think of me when you're on the beach with that parasol drink."

"Hope I don't have to."

"Ha, ha."

⌘⌘⌘

A little after two in the afternoon, Meredith loaded her bags onto a cart and pushed it to the opposite end of the Kahului terminal. As she moved through the thick humid air, she guessed her makeup must be running.

12

She found Island Air in a low-rise building, roofed but open on one side, and approached the counter.

Where were the trade winds? Her silk pantsuit clung to her skin. Her feet were swollen from the five-hour flight from SF and sticking to her stilettos. She fished in her red handbag for a tissue to blot her cheeks and forehead, and another to clean her oversized dark glasses. Where was the aroma of flowers she remembered? The air reeked of gasoline.

"Hana?" the clerk asked. Shuffling papers, she reached for Meredith's ticket.

"Please." Meredith lifted her bags onto the scale.

"We can't guarantee arrival. Storms are sudden."

"But it's clear," Meredith said, looking at the sky. "You can't guarantee arrival?" Perhaps she should rent a car and tackle the two-hour drive down the coast.

"The Hana airport has no radar. If cloud cover comes in, it's a no-go."

"What happens then?"

"When?"

"When cloud cover comes in," Meredith said, her tone edged with anger. She tapped her foot, cursing the humidity.

The clerk eyed her as though she were a blithering idiot. "If Hana is covered with cloud, the pilot turns around."

"And when is the next flight?"

"In the morning. Are you canceling, Ms. Campbell?"

Meredith dabbed her forehead with the tissue. "No, I'm not canceling."

Within the hour, she climbed a rope ladder and lowered her head as she stepped into a six-seater propjet. Two couples waited as Meredith found 1A and worked to buckle the shoulder strap into the lap belt. The pilot, her long dark hair pulled into a band, took her place in the cockpit and ran her fingers over the controls, checking and speaking into her headset. Meredith could see beyond her, past the computer screens and blinking panels, and out the high, curved windshield.

They taxied into position on the short runway, and Meredith braced herself for takeoff, wondering with some nervousness how puddle-jumpers like this ever managed to fly. She peered out her window, under the wing, a thrill shooting through her as she felt the momentum of the plane build, the engine roar and vibrate up her spine. She had never flown in one of these. A new experience. Something sexy about it too.

The plane lifted off, and Meredith watched the ground disappear beneath her. She watched the world below become small like a child's play village: the airport with its buildings and runways arranged at straight angles, the rooftops and green yards, the shops and parking lots, the schools and churches, the broad embracing farmlands. The motor leveled to a smooth hum, and they banked in an arc to the east, turned south, and flew low along a coastline of forested cliffs eroded by the sea. White foam crashed against black rock and red earth. Clouds hung over Haleakala to the west, and as the sun dropped behind them, silver rays shot through dark canyons and over green fields, fingers playing on the mountain birthed by the waters.

The plane flew smooth and low over the sea along the coast. Meredith watched for a minute, briefly entranced, drank from her water bottle, and checked her face in her slim compact. Her creamy skin glistened in the humidity, and there was a slight flush along her cheekbones. She examined her shadow and liner, and closed her compact with a satisfied sigh. She ran a brush through her hair so that it fell in silky waves, teasing her bare shoulders, and pulled out *Vogue* and a nail file. She hoped the hotel's spa was everything they said it was. She wanted a manicure and a facial for starters, and a full-body mud treatment wouldn't be a bad idea.

"That's where that fellow drowned," the woman behind her said to her companion.

Meredith looked out the window and saw a broad plateau jutting from the coast. High surf crashed against black rock.

"They never found the body," the man replied.

"Washed over the cliff?"

"Must have been some storm."

"Seems so peaceful now."

"That's the islands for you."

Meredith shivered and returned to her magazine, catching up on the Paris shows. Soon she felt the plane descend. As they approached a short runway, she looked through her window to dense forest sloping to the sea, the plane flying low, nearing the earth. Suddenly they dropped onto the pavement, rocked gently, and taxied toward a single-story building.

Bending, she climbed out of the cabin, down the rope ladder, onto the tarmac, and into the blazing sun. She approached the terminal, her handbag in one hand and her tote in the other. She glanced at her watch. Five o'clock. Seven, SF time. She hoped the hotel wasn't far. She was dying for a martini.

She retrieved her luggage and inquired at the desk about a taxi to the hotel. The deeply tanned clerk, smiling and nodding an enthusiastic welcome, pointed outside to a bright red trolley. Other passengers were loading their mismatched bags and climbing aboard. She raised her brows at the friendly clerk. He nodded and pointed again.

This is not an auspicious beginning, she thought as she walked toward the vehicle, her heels clicking. The driver set her luggage in the back. Was this an old fire engine? A cattle car? She climbed aboard and pulled a tissue from her bag to wipe the vinyl bench. Sitting down gingerly, she frowned at her wrinkled silk jacket. The truck jerked up the road, and she grabbed a chrome handrail. A moist wind blew through the open windows, sending her hair flying. *It's a bloody rain forest.* She peered at the lush growth on either side of the highway. *Parker didn't say anything about the Amazon.*

The engine whirred, chomped, and emitted strange guttural sounds. The driver tried to speak above the racket and the creaking of the side panels.

"This was built as a fire truck," he was saying. "It's a '39 Packard. I'd say it's in pretty good condition, all things considered."

Some of the passengers giggled and sighed with appreciation.

"Before 1850," he continued, "Hana Ranch was Hana Plantation. There was a grass shack and a mill run by oxen. Then it became part of the Ka'eleku Sugar Company. In 1944, the San Francisco businessman Paul Fagan bought all fourteen thousand acres of the plantation and founded Hana Ranch, replacing the sugar fields with white Herefords. Today you can see the cattle grazing all over the property."

15

Who cares?

But the driver's broad shoulders reminded her of Nick, and with renewed determination, she pictured him on a horse, riding through the waves, maybe wearing a Stetson.

She pulled out her cell and checked her messages. Nothing. It was still early, only forty-eight hours since she found him with *that woman* in *their* bed. She had been fortunate to get a flight out so quickly, to find a cancellation so soon.

How long would it take Nick to find her? Maybe a week, tops? She needed a tan, more workouts, and some spa time. A week, and Nick would be begging. He would find her, all right, and the sex would be better than ever. She smiled. Parker would let him know her location.

"In 1946," the driver explained, "Mr. Fagan created the first Hotel Hana-Maui—six rooms called the Ka'uiki Inn. It grew to become the wonderful hotel you will enjoy today, but first I'll make a loop through Hana town."

Hana town was no more than an intersection, Meredith thought, as they spluttered and bounced along. The driver pointed out the post office, the general store, and the local grill. He rattled up a circular drive and squeaked to a stop in front of a modest ranch-style building.

He jumped out and offered his thick hand to Meredith. She ignored him and stepped on the running board, then down to the pavement, her eyes scanning the open-air lobby. Parker said *posh*. It didn't look very posh to her.

A dark-skinned woman in a long floral dress approached the truck. She carried a tray of juice and napkins in a bed of flowers. "Welcome to Hotel Hana-Maui," she said with a wide white smile.

Three

A young porter drove Meredith and her luggage to her cabin in a golf cart. As they rolled down a paved path through acres of lawn descending to the sea, the boy pointed to the mountain behind them.

"Haleakala," he said. "Our volcano, ten thousand feet high." He smiled, glancing at her. "Not to worry, ma'am, it's been dormant for over eight hundred years."

They passed green-shingled cabins with wooden verandahs facing toward the sea.

Meredith nodded. "Lots of palms." She tried to sound cheerful. The boy wasn't bad looking. She wondered how old he was. He was probably part Hawaiian and good-looking in a preppy sort of way. He *must be dying to get out of here,* she thought.

He turned the cart abruptly and cut across a lawn. "They're coconut palms. The red plants with the long leaves are *ti* plants. Our dancers make their skirts from them. The bushes with the yellow flowers are plumeria, good for leis. What you smell, though, is jasmine and gardenia mostly."

Meredith breathed deeply. The air was fragrant and moist, holding promise.

They passed tennis courts and a huge lap pool.

"Been to Hana before?" the porter asked.

"No, I haven't."

He pulled up to a bungalow. "It's quiet here. Planning to do some work?"

"No," she said, glancing at him.

"Pleasure then?"

"Pleasure," she purred.

He grinned. His teeth were white and even, his skin smooth. His muscles tightened as he grabbed her bags.

She smiled back. "Yes," she repeated in her huskiest voice, "definitely pleasure."

He loaded her bags onto the timbered bed. "There's a Jacuzzi bathtub inside and a hot tub on the deck in back. And here's the control for the ceiling fan." He turned a wall dial and the blades began a slow whirl. He pointed to the open shutters on three sides of the room. "Natural air conditioning. Hope you enjoy yourself then, miss."

"I hope so too," she said with just the right innuendo.

"My name is Tony. If you need anything, anything at all, you just ask for Tony."

"I'll remember that, Tony," she said, raising a brow and meeting his eyes. "Bye for now." She pressed a five-dollar bill into his calloused palm.

She closed the door behind him and crossed to the back deck where the hot tub bubbled, its motor grinding. She leaned on the railing.

To her right, the sun was setting behind Haleakala, its rays shooting between gathering clouds. To her left, a pale blue sky met a dark blue sea. A wind whistled through the tall palms, and Meredith sighed. Her nagging feeling had returned. She needed to do something, catch some action.

There wasn't a soul in sight. The place was dead. She wondered how soon the spa would open in the morning. She stepped inside and dialed. "Closed for renovations? You've got to be kidding."

She began to unpack. Why had she come here? She was suddenly famished. She hadn't eaten since noon. She showered, changed into a skintight black tee and a skirt that rode low on her hips, showing off the diamond in her navel. She walked back up the path between torches flaming on poles, toward the bar and dining room.

"Parker," she barked into her cell as she stepped through the gathering dusk, "I hope you get this message. Your great hotel isn't so great, unless you like solitary confinement." Her phone went dead. No signal.

⌘⌘⌘

A storm came in that night and continued into the next day and evening. Water pounded the tin roofs of the cabins, drowning out the roar of the surf, as fierce gale winds drove the system over the island. Then the rain let up as though a faucet had been turned off.

The second night Meredith lay on the feather bed and listened to the storm ebb and flow, hoping the road might be passable in the morning. The desk clerk said it often flooded. Bored and nervous with unease, she couldn't take much more of this place.

She had spent the day wandering between the bar, the restaurant, and the two shops, one for "sundries" and one for "resort wear." She read every fashion magazine and bought a few bikinis. She tasted a sweet rum drink with a parasol and nearly choked. After that, the bartender had consoled her with excellent martinis. The hotel manager tried to calm her when she demanded to know why the spa was unfinished and the Wellness Center closed. He offered her the splendid heated pools. She looked at him with derision as the rain pelted the garden outside his office, and he assured her the storm would not last longer than a few more days.

"It's our rainy season," he said. "It's February."

"Find me a car," she demanded. "Your hotel is lovely. It's simply not what I expected. I need more people."

"I understand," he said, and Meredith sensed he did. "Few people come alone to Hana. It's a place for quiet, for meditation, and for...couples desiring privacy."

Now, in the giant bed, she waited for daylight, cursing the constant banging of the rain on the metal roof and the howling wind. The manager had promised the car for nine in the morning.

⌘ ⌘ ⌘

Her bags were packed by eight. She gulped a coffee and rode up the hill in Tony's cart. The boy loaded her luggage into the trunk of the rental.

"Maybe next time things be better," Tony said.

"Maybe next time." She managed a smile and slipped behind the wheel. Wailea would be sunny, the manager had assured her, so he had booked her a room at the Grand, a hotel that would be all she desired.

The rain battered the windshield as she drove out of Hana. She strapped on her seat belt, pushed the defog button, and switched on the wipers. Relieved to be on her way, she careened around hairpin turns, working up the coast one curve at a time, slowing to gawk at muddy rivers cascading through ravines and rushing under stone bridges. Never had she seen so much water—pouring from the skies, channeled into gorges, gushing through the forest. *What a place.*

Picturing the color photos in the Grand's brochure, she cut a bend too close and veered into the opposite lane. A horn blasted from an oncoming van. She turned sharply to the right and plowed into an abandoned roadside stand. The wooden shack splintered and cracked, and she heard something slide off the cliff to the sea below. Slowed by the impact, her car came to a halt amidst the rubble.

She leaned over the steering wheel and felt for broken bones. The windshield was covered in debris. She pushed the door open and found herself facing a pair of dripping jeans.

"You okay, ma'am?" A heavyset dark-skinned man peered down at her. He offered her a thick arm.

She ignored the arm and looked up into the mist. The rain had stopped.

"I think so, considering you nearly ran me off the road."

"You crossed over, ma'am."

She tried to start the engine. Her wheels spun.

"You're on the edge of a cliff," he said. "That's a good five hundred feet to the sea. I don't think this car's going anywhere, ma'am, at least, nowhere you want to go."

She grabbed her handbag, reached for his arm, and pulled herself out. "But you've got a van."

His chest was massive, and he wore a yellow shirt open at the neck. A silver cross rested on moist skin. "Goin' the other way, ma'am, but happy to give you a lift."

"I have to get to Wailea. I'll pay you." Her head was beginning to throb. She turned toward the front of the car and gasped. The wheels dangled in midair. Her car had rammed straight through the shed.

"You can't keep me from getting fired, ma'am. I need to go to

Hana, the other direction."

Meredith felt faint as she faced him. "This can't be happening." *Back to Hana? How could she?*

"I'll radio for help and you can wait here, but lookin' at your front end...." He peered at the cliff edge through the rubble. "In fact, ma'am, I would advise you to stand back *right now.* Anything in the trunk you need?"

"My luggage..." She unlatched the lid.

"Stand back, ma'am!" He towered behind her, pushed her aside, and grabbed the bags. As the rear weight lifted, the car inched forward and slipped over the side, crunching and squeaking, taking timber and brush with it.

"No," she said in barely a whisper, stunned, as the car disappeared, plunging to the sea. "Do something!" she cried, turning to the man. "Why did you take those bags out? It's your fault, you fool!" She patted her pockets, found her cell phone, and punched 911. No response. The out-of-range signal beeped.

The man returned to his van. "I'll radio the police. We need to make a report."

Meredith sat on her luggage and stared at her phone. The mist was now a drizzle, and her wet hair clung to her face. Her silk jacket was ruined. She wanted to cry.

"Did you get the police?" she asked as he returned with a blanket.

"Come along, ma'am. I'll drive you to the hotel. They agreed to take your report there."

"My report?"

"Your car plunged off the cliff. This qualifies, I should think, ma'am, as a traffic accident."

Meredith allowed him to help her into the front passenger seat. He threw her bags in the back. She stared straight ahead, feeling as though the last days of the world were upon her. How she would survive another hour on this island was beyond her imagination.

"My name's Patrick Kaelani, ma'am. Pleased to meet you."

"Campbell. Meredith Campbell." At least she still had her luggage. She sure needed a drink.

⌘ ⌘ ⌘

The fellow at the other end of the bar eyed Meredith and motioned her over. His graying hair fell to his shoulders, and a jagged scar ran up his jaw line. Bloodshot eyes leered from a pockmarked face. He wore a flowered shirt and a gold chain around his neck. His chest hair was a jungle of black and silver. He was drinking shots of something amber.

She had been given her old bungalow as the rain continued to pour, closing down the road to Kahului. She had made her police report, changed into dry clothes, and sat in the lobby, scanning old headlines. It was noon, and finally time for a pre-lunch cocktail. The roads were still flooded. It might be days before they opened again.

"What'll you have, young lady?" he asked as she slipped onto the stool next to him. A snake, coiled on a skull, was tattooed on his leathery arm, and needle marks riddled his wrist. "I'm a Scotch man myself."

"Vodka martini, dry, straight up, twist."

"You've got it." He nodded to the barman.

"Nasty weather," she commented.

"Nasty, but normal." He stared at her breasts.

"Are you stuck here too?" She tried not to look him in the eyes. He was too creepy.

"I suppose you could say that, but it's not a bad place to be stuck. This is a great hotel. Never stayed here, mind you."

"Of course, it's a great hotel."

"Are you alone?"

She glanced at the veiled lids, the haggard face. He reminded her of an old rock star.

"I'm meeting someone." A partial truth. A half lie.

"Want a little company while you wait? I've got some good stuff, grade-A. We could have a little party and pass the time. Let me introduce myself. I'm Woody."

"Meredith. What've you got?"

"A little weed," he said under his breath. "I supply the area, and folks are grateful. The high school chicks are especially grateful. Would *you* be grateful?"

She shivered. "How'd you manage to get here in all this rain?"

"Flew, naturally. Got my own plane."

"Really?" She looked at him with increased interest.

"Made it between storms."

"Could you fly out again? I'd pay you."

"Not in this weather, baby." He leaned toward her. "How about letting me see your room? I hear they're mighty nice. Like to see that hot tub too." He ran his finger lightly along her arm.

She flinched, and hoped he didn't notice. "You promise to fly me out, rain or shine, and you can see my room." He might be useful.

He grinned, showing yellow teeth. "Well, honey, now that's a promise." He guided her to the door, his hand on the small of her back. "I've got a sweet deal waiting in Honolulu I'd hate to miss. But hey, how about lunch first?"

She bought him lunch in the verandah restaurant and kept his propjet in mind when they ordered their second bottle of wine. He was her ticket, and she wouldn't forget it. By the time she settled the bill, the rain had stopped, and they staggered down the path, Woody swinging and swigging the half-full second bottle, past the massive pool and Wellness Center, through the gardens, and across the lawns to her cottage.

She turned on the hot tub, and they stretched out on the chaise lounges, faces to the sky, catching the sun descending to the mountain. An enormous black cloud soon blew in and the wind picked up. "Another front comin'," he said, his eyes closed. "That tub's goin' to be mighty nice." He glanced at her body.

They stripped and sat on the molded plastic in the bubbling water, puffing and trading a reefer. Lightning flashed over the sea, and Meredith admitted things were looking better. The alcohol and the drugs floated through her mind, coloring the humid air with distant hope.

When they tumbled onto the bed, he was a little rough, fast and piercing, and for a moment she regretted her bargain. Then he rolled off and passed out. She stared at his brown bony body with disgust and crawled onto the couch.

The rain poured on and off all night, slamming the deck outside and the skylight above. The wind howled.

Tomorrow she would fly out of here.

⌘⌘⌘

The hotel trolley dropped them off at the airport in the gray of early dawn. The storm had let up, but the skies remained threatening.

The clerk behind the counter frowned. "We're closed," he said nervously. "No flying today. High winds."

Meredith stared at the landing strip, her heart sinking. "Are you sure? We're not going far."

Woody eyed the clerk threateningly. "Sorry, my friend, *you* may be closed, but *I'm* flying." He opened his jacket and rested his hand on a revolver wedged in his jeans.

The young man raised his hands. "Of course it's your choice, sir. He opened a drawer and pulled out a paper. "You'll need to sign off, if you would, please, sir."

"Load the plane," Woody said as he scrawled his name.

Meredith watched the two men haul her luggage along with Woody's boxes.

"Can I ask what's in the boxes?" the clerk said as they returned. "For my records?"

"No, you sure can't." Woody grabbed Meredith's arm tightly. "Ready, little lady? We'd better go before the next storm hits. All we need is a half-hour window to get to Kahului."

They boarded the small twin engine and Meredith took the co-pilot's seat. She looked back into the cabin. Two long fuel tanks, the tubular shape of bombs, lay side by side where the seats had been.

"Sometimes I need the extra gas," Woody said as they taxied down the runway, "for quick getaways, if ya know what I mean." He winked at her.

"Sure." She told herself it was none of her business what side of the law he was on. He was getting her out of there.

Woody handed her earplugs. "You better wear these and strap up."

She fastened her belt and watched the rain pelt the windshield. The plane lifted into the wind and rolled slightly. The engine roared.

"How can you see where you're going?" she shouted as she inserted the earplugs.

"I don't. That's what these dials are for. We'll be within radar soon. The Hana airport still doesn't have radar."

She swallowed, her throat dry, and gripped the armrests. The plane struggled against the storm, a manmade machine pushing against the natural world. They flew steadily for a few minutes, and she watched the dials blink and the arrows waver. She tried to picture Nick, but his image had faded. So much had happened since she saw him last.

They dropped, lurched, and Woody swore.

"Lost an engine," he said. "Sorry, baby, but we've got to land." He scanned the horizon through the slanting rain, his face white.

Meredith peered into swirling gray as the plane tilted, suspended in the quiet.

"The other one's dead too!" Woody cried.

I'm going to die, she thought. The plane dropped and her insides churned. What would dying be like? "Are we crashing?" she screamed, her voice hoarse, choked.

"Just hold tight, lady, and shut up. There's a plateau up here a ways. I've used it before. Hold tight and shut up!"

In the eerie silence, they floated through the clouds, pushed by the wind, and Meredith thought of her father. She was five, and they were heading up Seventh toward Central Park. Her mother was there too, and Meredith ran between them, trying to keep up. They lifted her by her hands and laughed. The sidewalk flew under her feet, and she laughed too. What happened? They were a family once. Did all families fall apart like that? Did she know of one that hadn't?

The clouds parted, revealing a flat peninsula with black-rock cliffs. The sea rose in giant swells below.

"We're falling into the sea," she screamed. "We're going to drown!"

"Shut up, lady, just shut up."

She braced herself for the impact, thinking, *Please, don't let it hurt.*

Woody maneuvered closer to the plateau, and Meredith closed her eyes. She heard the crunching of metal and the bump, bump of the plane on the ground. Her seatbelt tightened against her chest, and her head slammed against something hard. The last thing she remembered was a loud boom in the distance and searing pain.

Four

The morning was brilliantly clear when they found the plane, the air washed by the rain. A few clouds hovered over the mountain.

Tutu Nani-lei sat in her swinging chaise on the back verandah. Softly humming an old hula tune, she had settled Lucy's crocheted headband over the child's ears so that it nestled in her dark curls, and the little girl in her yellow sundress ran through the grass, picking daisies and wild lilies, her bare feet sure of their territory. Eli, their chocolate lab, and Alabar, their graying shepherd, ran with her, and once again Nani sensed the happiness of renewed life, after a dark night of rushing winds and thunderous rains. She had awakened early in the morning, sure she had heard a loud clap of thunder, but now all was calm.

The old woman looked beyond the plateau out to the sea and prayed the storm had not taken any victims as often happened along this rocky coast. She shivered, recalling the tourists pulled out by a high wave only last week. The sea was beautiful but dangerous, and like all of nature, a force with no regard for man. In this sense the ancients rightly feared the power of the natural world. Her husband, Lou, God rest his soul, had drowned in a fishing accident, the entire crew with him, and he was an experienced sailor. But today the air held only sweetness after the drenching and the winds, and Nani rocked in the lounge, the twittering of sparrows and the rustling of palms soothing her senses. She dropped her heavy lids for a moment....

"Nani, Nani!" A small hand shook her leg. How long had she been napping? Eli licked her face, and Alabar sat attentive, his ears bristling.

She pulled herself up, gently nudged the lab away, and focused on Lucy. The child looked so like her mother Maria at that age, her face holding that same patient persistence, and Nani started, once again caught off guard. Another sea tragedy. Would they never end? Two years wasn't enough to forget Maria's drowning. *Maria.*

"Nani!" Lucy cried again.

"What is it, child?" Nani saw that Lucy's bangs needed trimming. The child's brown eyes were full of worry.

The old tutu ran her thick hand over the headband, tenderly parted the bangs, and slipped a stray curl behind Lucy's ear. "Why you so troubled? Nani's here. Sit on Nani's lap, and we make story."

"Nani, come, come...you must...," Lucy lisped, her voice urgent. She pulled on her arm.

Nani lifted herself from the swing and allowed the child to lead her across the field to the cliffs, down the wooded slope toward the sea. A wisp of smoke curled into the air above the plumeria trees. She smelled burning metal.

As they drew near, Nani's eyes narrowed. The wreckage of a smoldering plane could be seen through the undergrowth. There was something red in the grass.

"Lucy, go to the house and bring your papa, now, hurry...and take Eli and Alabar."

Lucy obeyed, and Nani turned toward the wreckage. Twisted metal steamed in the moist air. Clearly, there had been an explosion. The red looked to be a woman's handbag. No one could have survived this fire, no one who remained in the plane. And the rain must have put the fire out just as quickly as it started.

She circled the charred fuselage, hitching up her skirts, stepping carefully through the grass, searching for signs of life. *Maria's plane must have been small like this,* she thought, the one that crashed in the bay. Young people had no fear, no sense, no understanding of what has happened to those gone before. Would they not listen until it was too late? She swallowed her grief-anger, breathed deeply, flattened her palms together, and looked to the heavens, readying herself for what she might find.

About ten yards from the wreckage, a woman's leg oozed blood. It angled awkwardly, pinned under a long piece of metal.

Nani paused. Maybe, she thought, she should wait for Henry. He would know what to do. And yet, if the woman was alive....

Nani moved closer. The lady lay still. Her face was gashed, and the blood had caked. Was she breathing?

Nani placed a finger against the woman's neck and felt a slow pulse. "Oh Lordy, what now?" With all her strength, she pushed at the metal. It moved slightly and rocked back to its position. She stood aside, her hands on her hips.

She tried again, her thick hands on the rough steel, shoving and lifting. It moved a bit more and fell back again.

She sighed and knelt in the grass, slipping the bloody head onto her lap.

"Wake up, little lady. You going to be okay, Nani will see to that." She stroked the matted hair. "We're gonna wait for Henry. Henry will help. Sweet Jesus, let this little lady be okay. She's too young to be dying, while I'm too old to be living. It's not right, sweet Jesus. You know it's not right."

She heard Henry's step and looked up.

He wore his bathrobe, the blue one she stitched for Christmas, and he had pulled on the galoshes kept by the door. His high forehead glistened, and his wire-rimmed glasses caught the sun.

"Is she alive?" He stared at the woman lying in Nani's lap.

"I think so. She has a weak pulse. Her leg's pinned down, Henry. I couldn't lift the metal."

He pushed the steel up and over, freeing her. "I told Lucy to wait in the house."

"Good."

Henry looked over the wreckage. "Where's the pilot? Did you find anyone else?"

"There's not much of anything left here, Henry. Hurry now. She may not have much time."

"We need to move her inside. I'll bring the hammock from the shed and some sheeting."

"Call Sammy. He's in Hana today."

When he returned, they wrapped the woman's face and leg, slid her onto the hammock, and carried her slowly through the tall grass, up to Hana-lani, past Lucy sitting on the kitchen stoop, her eyes wide, sucking her thumb.

⌘ ⌘ ⌘

Tutu Nani-lei stood by the bamboo bed in the upstairs guest room, keeping watch with the dogs. Eli slept on the throw rug, his head cradled in his huge paws, and Alabar sat alert, on guard. It had been three hours since they lowered the woman onto the deep feather mattress, but she had not yet awakened.

They had taken her to the clinic, where Nani's grandnephew, Dr. Samuel Tagami, X-rayed her skull and cleaned the wounds on her leg and face. He stitched the skin together, smoothed on ointment, and wrapped gauze strips about her face like a mummy. The woman moaned and mumbled but didn't regain full consciousness.

The driver's license in the red bag said she was Meredith Campbell of San Francisco, but no one answered the home number listed with the DMV. The clinic was full, so they sent her to Hana-lani, as they had done with others. Sammy said to call when she woke up, and Nani intended to be there when she did.

The police had searched the area and pronounced the pilot dead, sounding relieved when they were able to identify him, glad he would no longer trouble Hana. They said he was a bad sort, and now Nani wondered what this young woman had to do with such a man, seeming so innocent as she slept. Her matted hair was golden, and her skin, what could be seen, was the color of fresh cream. Her long dark lashes rested on her cheeks like mini fan ferns, and when Nani saw movement under the lids, she knew the girl was dreaming.

She raised the quilt to the bandaged face. It was a sad business, but Nani had learned a few things during the war and would nurse Miss Campbell as best she could. She had exiled Lucy to other rooms, but soon she must allow her to help. For it was worse for Lucy to be separated from her tutu than to see the bloody wounds.

Nani had bathed the pale body in rose water and carefully slipped one of her own muslin nightgowns over it, gently pulling up the cotton past the red-painted toenails, up the slim legs, over the thin torso to the chin, tying the ribbons above each shoulder. She said a prayer she learned long ago for her children when they had measles and flu, colds and chicken pox. *O heavenly Father, watch with us, we pray thee, over the sick child for whom our prayers are offered, and grant that she may be restored to that perfect health, which it is thine alone to give.* Each time she prayed the prayer she saw in her mind her mother's white leather book with the multicolored satin markers lying between the tissue pages. The healing prayer had a green one in the fold, green like the rainforest.

Nani watched the young woman, her heart full.

Henry had fled to his study when Sammy and the police took over. He would be no help with Lucy, and Nani sensed the vision of the woman triggered nightmares of Maria. The old grandmother shook her head. She patted the shepherd, then stroked the lab, who looked up at her from time to time with his dark, liquid eyes. This was a sad business indeed, she thought. This young woman would hurt her grandson even more. She would be either a blessing or a curse, of that Nani was sure. For once, she was glad Henry hid in his study.

His long hours, writing whatever he wrote, removed him, as though he were on another island. When father and daughter dined at the long koa table, the silence was met only by Nani's light chatter as she told Lucy the stories of their people. Henry's wounds were deep and she would not judge, but she must help Lucy heal. And now, it seemed, she must help this young woman heal. One must rise to the occasion, as her mother often said, for it was simply the right thing to do and, never forget, duty is the conscience of love.

Nani touched the young hand, stroking the smooth white skin stretched over long delicate fingers. She wondered what her face had looked like before it was covered in blood and then bandages, and what had brought her to Hana. Each person had a story, she knew, a unique beginning, middle, and end, and she longed to know each one. One day, when she traveled on, she would know them all, she was sure of it.

She lowered her large frame into the rocking chair her papa had carved and reached for her needlework, an embroidery pattern of palms and hibiscus and bluebirds that would one day cover thick cotton batting. She angled the lamp to see better and squinted through thick glasses, picking up where she left off. The quilt was for Lucy. Lucy's baptism was to be this Easter Day, at last. It had taken two years of nagging Henry, and he had given in, praise God.

Had it really been two years since Henry and Lucy had arrived in the pouring rain? As she poked the needle with its red thread into the ecru cotton, she could see the day like it was yesterday...the day Maria's husband and daughter had entered her empty house, and her life, suddenly filling both. Cousins and aunts, nieces and nephews, grandchildren of all sorts had come and gone over the years, but lately Hana-lani had been quietly empty, as if waiting for that moment in the pouring rain.

⌘ ⌘ ⌘

Lucy's yellow slicker had been wet and dripping, the hood pulled up over the curls about her face. She wore a pink backpack with Tinker Bell painted in sparkles.

"Welcome home, Henry," Nani said. "Your old room is ready. Is this our little Lucy?"

"Lucy can have my old room." He was gray with fatigue. Nani could tell he had not slept for a long time, and fifty was no longer young.

"Hello, Lucy." Nani crouched to her eye level.

The child looked confused, afraid, tired.

"She can't hear well, Tutu Nani. She was born with a hearing impediment."

Nani glanced at Henry reprovingly. "I didn't know." She took Lucy's tiny hand and led her inside.

Henry pulled out a headband and slipped the ends over Lucy's ears. "This helps. I took it off so she could sleep on the plane. She doesn't like it."

Nani bent down again. "Now, little one, my name is Nani. What's yours?"

"Lucy. My name's Lucy Maria Fitzhugh, and I'm four, almost five." She raised an open hand, fingers splayed triumphantly, and ran into the living room, dripping a trail of water behind her.

"Henry, let me look at you. Let me hold my boy again."

"Nani," he moaned, his voice choked with sorrow. He reached down to her, and she wrapped her arms around his back, feeling his shoulder blades.

"It will get better, Henry, you'll see." But her own heart throbbed so. Would it get better?

Henry unpacked while Lucy watched Nani reheat fish stew over the gas stove, stirring with a wooden spoon.

"Where's Mommy?" Lucy asked as she climbed on a stool.

"She's gone away for a time, little one."

Nani knitted covers for the headband in pink and yellow and blue. She sewed Lucy flowered dresses and took her to Hasegawa's. She taught her to help with the house, to set and clear the table, and to wash the dishes, standing on a stepstool so she could reach the sink.

⌘ ⌘ ⌘

Now Nani waited with the dogs, watching the hurt woman in the bamboo bed. Alabar lay against Eli, breathing heavily and dozing. When Lucy was grown, the old tutu could pass into the great sleep. How tired she was of late.

Nani removed her glasses and placed them on the nightstand. She turned out the light, folded her hands on the quilt in her lap, and dozed as well.

Five

Meredith blinked. The room was bright and the images blurry. Multiple heads, noses, ears. Her own head pounded, a throbbing that started at the base of her neck, spread through the back of her skull, and pushed into her temples, like a balloon expanding under her skin. Within that pain, or maybe on its edge, deep near her right cheekbone, fire burned. The same burning ran through her thigh muscle. She tried to move, but found she was bound tightly by bed sheets. Something wet lapped her hand.

The images came into focus, and she saw a young face, a child, she thought, with a pink headband and long dark hair and wide brown eyes that stared back, blinking too. A large dog, a lab, licked her fingers with his coarse pink tongue. Suddenly the child grinned and jumped up and down. Meredith's head pounded harder with the movement.

"Nani! Nani! She's awake! She's awake!"

The dogs barked, loud claps shooting through her temple.

"We need the tea!" the child screamed.

"Calm down, little one, let old Tutu see for herself. Remember your manners."

A larger form loomed over Meredith, blocking out the light. She tried to sit up. Who was this? Where was she? The weathered brown face smiled, showing gums. Thick fingers patted an ivory cross on a dark chest. Voluminous purple floral. Another dog, a shepherd, nosed in next to the lab.

"Aloha, Miss Campbell. We are your hosts, *mea ho'okipa*. Don't you worry, child; you'll be just fine." The old woman nodded sagely.

"Where am I?" Meredith could barely whisper.

"You're at Hana-lani, baby, Hana-lani. Your plane crashed. You're lucky to be alive."

Meredith touched the gauze bandage about her head. "*Oh my*

God."

"*Be praised*," Nani said. "Your face will heal, dear."

"My face...oh no..." She moved her fingers over the bandage, desperately searching for skin. Her cheek throbbed.

"The rest of you is okay too, just a few stitches in that leg there."

"A mirror. Give me a mirror. Please." Meredith looked about the room. Muslin curtains hung from bamboo poles. Her red handbag sat next to a Tiffany lamp on a pine dresser. Primitive art, unframed, was taped to wood-paneled walls. She pushed herself up on her elbows.

"Slow down, dearie, slow down. You had a bad fall."

Trying to sit up sent a stab of pain through her skull. She slid back into the coarse sheets and gratefully rested her head on the pillows.

"That's better, dear. You sure you want a mirror?"

"Please...what day is it?"

"It's Wednesday, February twenty-fifth, Ash Wednesday, as a matter of fact."

"What happened?" she asked. Her mind reached back, searching her memory.

"Lucy found you, or rather she found the wrecked plane, on the edge of our cliff. I'm sorry, my dear, but the pilot..."

"The pilot? What happened to the pilot? Where's my luggage?"

"The pilot," Nani said, her eyes narrowing, "died in the crash. He left just enough for the police to identify him. I'm sorry. Was he your friend?"

Meredith recalled the withered body sprawled on the bed. "No. And my bags? Anything left of my bags?"

"Just one left." The old woman pointed to the dresser. "You're Meredith Campbell, I believe. I'm Nani-lei Brown, and this is Lucy. We're pleased to meet you."

"I'm Lucy Maria Fitzhugh, and I'm six, almost seven!" the child cried. She held up both hands, fingers splayed.

Meredith winced. She took their hands, first the large thick one, dry and chapped, then the tiny thin one, moist and smooth. The child stared through thick black lashes.

"Pleased likewise," Meredith said, "but how did I get *here?*"

"The clinic discharged you," Nani said. "Not enough beds, so we'll take care of you for a time."

"But—"

"You need to heal," Nani said, patting her arm, "and we're happy to have you here at Hana-lani for as long as that takes."

"But my cell. Did you find my cell? Everyone's in my cell."

Nani handed her the slim silver phone.

Meredith tapped the pad. "Dead."

"Anyone I can call for you?" The old woman sounded genuinely concerned.

Meredith paused, a sudden fear racing through her. No one must see her like this. *No one.* "Not yet." Nick could wait—she didn't want him near her now—and Parker couldn't keep a secret. Meredith slowly realized she had no one she could call.

"Here's the mirror."

Meredith held the tarnished glass to her face and gasped. A wide bandage wrapped her right cheekbone up to her forehead and was secured in place with strips about her head. She dropped the mirror on the bed and stared at the beamed ceiling. She may as well have died with that pilot.

"Drink this, dear." Nani held a cup of water to Meredith's lips, and she sipped slowly. "You rest now. I'm calling the doctor. And we'll bring you something to eat." The woman and child trooped out.

Meredith gazed at the pine ceiling with its two-by-fours and warped timber. She moved carefully in the sheets, testing out her body, but could not find a comfortable position. Her leg still burned, and her head pounded. She closed her eyes and dozed.

Within the hour Nani returned with a tray of mushy food that looked like pureed meat and vegetables. Lucy carried a mug of strong-smelling tea, balancing it carefully. She set it on the bedside table.

"It's Noni tea," the child said. "I made it myself!"

A doorbell rang in the distance, and Lucy ran off.

"She did make it." The old woman handed Meredith the cracked mug. "She knows how to make it now, such a bright child."

"What is it?" Meredith asked.

"Indian mulberry. Hawaiians have used the leaves for centuries to make healing-tea. We add a little honey to ours."

Meredith sipped the strong liquid. It tasted like medicine, she thought, but had a curious sweetness to it. Suddenly hungry, she reached for the bowl and carefully spooned the pulpy vegetables into her mouth. Sweet potatoes and carrots? Sage?

Nani nodded. "Good girl."

Lucy returned, leading a short young man wearing khakis and a powder blue polo shirt. He was clean-shaven and had the powerful bearing of a man at ease with himself.

"I'm Dr. Tagami, Ms. Campbell," he said, taking her hand in both of his, "but everyone calls me Sammy. I was your doctor at the clinic. I brought you here. Nani-lei Brown will care for you. She's an excellent nurse." He smiled fondly at the old woman.

"Shouldn't I be in a hospital?"

"We don't have one in Hana. The nearest is Kahului, over fifty miles away, but your injuries, amazingly enough, don't merit moving you. You were a lucky lady."

He felt her pulse, checking his watch, his touch gentle but firm. He was attractive, in a plain way, with tight muscles and hairless arms. His almond eyes crinkled in concern. He nodded and patted her hand. "You'll be okay now that you're awake." He turned to Nani. "The resemblance is remarkable, Tutu."

"She does look a little like her, Sammy, even with the bandages, but never you worry about that."

He stared at Meredith as though she were someone else.

"Thank you, Dr. Tagami...er...Sammy," she said, confused.

He smiled. "You're welcome, Ms. Campbell. Forgive me, but you remind me of a close relative who passed on awhile back. Now tell me, do you know what day it is?"

"Wednesday."

"And can you count to ten?"

She mumbled the numbers, rolling her eyes.

"Just testing, miss. Do you know where you are?"

"Maui."

"Close enough."

"Hana."

"Good." He tapped her knees and feet. "Responding okay."

Lucy pulled at his pant leg. "Uncle Sammy, Uncle Sammy, will you make the pretty lady well? Please, Uncle Sammy!"

"Quiet, child, manners, remember...," Nani said.

He lifted Lucy onto his hip and looked into her eyes. "Ms. Campbell will be fine," he whispered. He set her down.

He turned to Meredith. "You need a few more days of bed rest. You'll have headaches and might feel dizzy, even a little woozy. And some pain around the wounds. That's all normal. If you have any other symptoms, let me know right away."

"But what about my face?" She touched the bandages carefully with her fingertips.

"I can see you'd be worried, a pretty lady like yourself, but give it time." He reached for his bag.

"How much time?"

"You're young. Maybe six weeks." He handed Nani two vials of pills. "These are for the pain and any possible infection. Have her take them with food. And they'll help her sleep."

Meredith groaned. "Will I be scarred?"

"Let's say you'll have a small souvenir of a large miracle," he said as he packed his satchel. "You're a very lucky lady, miss." He led Lucy out the door.

Not too encouraging, Meredith thought. *Lucky lady? He's got to be kidding.*

⌘ ⌘ ⌘

She slept on and off, waking to see the old woman and the little girl by her bed as they told stories or sang hymns, the dogs snoring or panting, their long tongues dangling or licking her hand. Sometimes the child stroked Meredith's arms with her finger or tapped the polished nails with her own tiny ones. Meredith learned not to move her head, propped at an angle on three pillows. Nani helped her to the bathroom and washed her with a sweet-smelling lavender soap. She felt lightheaded when she stood, as though her legs might buckle, but slowly her world steadied. They brought her meals on bamboo trays.

She daydreamed or dreamed, she wasn't sure which, as the day merged into the night and back into day....

She was nine and wearing her pink leotard with the fanning organza, the soft slippers with matching pompoms, taking her place with the other girls, poised, toe pointed straight, one arm on her hip, one arm arcing over her head. The stage was dark, and the heavy curtain closed. As it opened slowly, a bright spotlight blinded her, the audience a large black hole. The familiar music began, a waltz, and she waited for the beat, the signal to follow the others in the dance, as she searched the dark crowd for her mother. Earlier backstage, her mother had dressed her, attending to details, and now Meredith found her, in the front row, her eyes wide, her form leaning forward, watching each movement. Her mother would remember every bow, step, and wave of her daughter's fingers. For her mother had been so perfect—perfect hair, dress, clothes—that it was natural she would expect perfection. Meredith would be perfect like her mother, for her mother....

Meredith dozed. On a low table by the window, an ill-shaped vase, splashed with blue and yellow, held flowers, and each day the little girl added to it. Sometimes the old woman rocked in her chair, humming.

At times Meredith slept deeply, as though drinking from a well. When she awoke, she rarely remembered who or where she was or why. A filmy haze clouded her thoughts, thoughts that meandered through the room.

She wondered what her mother was doing in Paris, what the models were wearing. Meredith had been pretty, but not pretty enough. All the dance lessons, the makeup and fashion lessons that would create the girl chosen to set the standards of beauty for her peers, indeed, for the world—all those lessons had been for nothing. Meredith had never been thin enough, never tall enough. Her features weren't quite what they needed that season. How many agencies had they visited? How many applications and photo shoots? And while she heard her mother's words, *"I love you, sweetie, you know I do,"* all the fussing and changing and fuming and frowning said something different. At least *now* her mother fussed and fumed over others....

One afternoon Meredith suddenly woke with a new energy. "What day is it?"

The old woman pulled herself up from her rocker and set down her needlework. "Why, it's Sunday, my dear."

"What Sunday?"

"Sunday the twenty-ninth of February, 2004. It's been five days you've been here at Hana-lani."

"A leap year day?" What would her astrologer say about that?

"It sure is, sweetie. Are you feeling better?" She turned to Lucy. "You see, Sammy was right. She would suddenly be better and she is."

"She's better!" the child screamed.

Meredith winced. "*God—*"

"*Be praised,*" Nani replied. "Manners, Lucy, manners."

Meredith eyed the old woman, thinking she must be one of those religious nuts. What kind of place was this? "I need to use the phone."

"Can you manage the stairs?" Nani asked.

"I'll try."

Nani gathered her quilting things and paused at the door. "Come down for dinner, Miss Campbell, six o'clock, and you can use the telephone then. There are clothes in the closet. You need anything, need help with the stairs, ring this." She set a tarnished silver bell on the bedside table. "There's a clock here next to the bell."

"But can't you bring me a phone?"

"Ring the bell, and we'll help you down the stairs, won't we, Lucy?"

Lucy nodded, adjusting her headband.

"The telephone's in the entry," Nani said. "It doesn't always work, but you might get lucky."

Six

Meredith gripped the smooth banister with one hand and Nani's arm with the other, taking one step at a time. Lucy descended in front of her, moving backwards, watching with her dark eyes. At the foot of the stairs the dogs paced, tapping the wood floor. Meredith reached the bottom step, and Nani shooed the dogs away.

A shadowy room was off to the left. Straight ahead the entry was planked and gleaming. Hats and coats hung from wooden knobs, rubber boots were lined up below. She spotted the black phone on the wall opposite. Aromas of garlic and shellfish wafted from the right. She stepped cautiously in her bare feet, floating in a billowing muumuu, the breezes blowing up and over her naked legs and torso. Her underwear was gone with the crash, and now the soft air tickled her skin.

She had examined her face in the cracked hand mirror when her bandages were changed. Two long and ragged cuts remained. Would she need plastic surgery?

Her hosts waited. She pulled the scuffed handset from the wall phone. "No dial tone." She held the instrument with an outstretched hand as though it were guilty.

Nani took the handset and placed it in its cradle. "Often happens here. Try later."

They stepped into the dining room. Through tall windows, Meredith glimpsed a vegetable garden, and beyond, the mountain, Haleakala. A mahogany sideboard, like her grandmother's in Brooklyn, only covered with a rustic cloth, stood against the opposite wall. Bright watercolors, which she now recognized as probably the child's efforts, were randomly tacked above. A long plank table occupied the length of the room.

A pale man, middle-aged, sat at the far end of the table, reading a slim, leather-bound volume. He wore wire-rimmed glasses, and dark circles shadowed his eyes. His mustache and trim beard made him look like an artist or academic, Meredith thought, her curiosity piqued. He wore a wedding ring, a plain gold band. His freckled fair skin contrasted to the smooth dark skin of the old woman and child. *Could they possibly be related?* Meredith wondered.

"Miss Campbell," Nani said, "may I present my grandson, Dr. Henry Tennyson Fitzhugh."

"Hi." Meredith sat down, glancing at her cotton gown with embarrassment. She touched her bandaged face nervously.

The man raised wary bloodshot eyes, nodded, and returned to his book.

Nani took the seat opposite Henry, next to Meredith, and Lucy climbed into the chair next to Henry. Two empty chairs on each side separated the couples.

"Your grandson?" Meredith could not conceal her surprise.

Nani eyed Henry's reading at the table with disapproval. "He's part of my *ohana*, my extended family," she explained. "He married my granddaughter, Maria, may her soul rest in peace. He lives here now with their daughter, Lucy. Forgive his manners."

"He's a doctor?" Meredith said quietly, eyeing Henry ,who seemed not to be aware of them.

"He's a professor-doctor. Used to teach at the university, my smart Henry." Nani nodded with pride.

Meredith considered the relationships as Nani passed a bowl of fish stew, a platter of fresh rolls, and a saucer of butter. She ladled the stew into her bowl and glanced sideways at Henry, who continued to read while buttering his bread.

Nani flattened her palms together and bowed her head. Lucy did the same. "Lord, we thank you for this food, and for this day and for this time together, and for this little lady's healing. We praise thy name, O Lord, for all thy glorious bounty! A...men."

"Amen!" Lucy cried as she clapped her hands and grinned at her father.

"Softly, little one," Nani said. "Lucy picked flowers, Henry."

Henry laid an embossed bookmark in the fold, set his book down, and reached for the stew. "So you picked flowers, Lucy?" he asked with apparent effort. He ladled a portion into his daughter's bowl.

"I did!" She pulled from her lap a posy of purple blossoms.

Henry examined them. "Why, those are princess flowers, from the glory-bush."

"Princess flowers?" She swung her legs against her chair...bump, bump, bump.

"Because they're pretty as a princess," he said, "just like you."

"*She's* a princess, I think!" Lucy pointed to Meredith. "Look at her hair!"

"Hardly." Meredith flashed a half-smile at Henry and winced as pain stabbed her cheek. "Mr. Fitzhugh," she began, "I want to thank you for taking me in.... I understand you saved my life." She wondered what his weakness was. Every man had a tender spot.

He looked up briefly and focused on Nani. "I'm not the one to thank. It was Tutu Nani who found you."

Nani smacked her food between her gums. "Lucy found her."

"I did, I did!" Lucy cried, clearly pleased. "With Eli and Alabar!"

The child was feeding herself with her fingers, and something from the stew glistened on the edges of her lips. Not only was she loud, Meredith thought, she was messy. Typical.

"Your napkin, Lucy," Nani said. "Use your silverware, and mind your manners."

Lucy bunched her napkin and swiped at her chin. She grabbed a fork and pitched it into the stew.

The dogs had settled under the table. One of them sniffed at Meredith's ankle, and a cold nose moved up her calf. *This is too much.*

Nani passed a wooden bowl of dressed greens. "Spinach leaves from the garden. Even in February, we have fresh greens, and with papaya seed dressing, Mama's recipe."

Meredith tried to ignore the wet nose, now settling on her toes. She kept her eyes away from the child's goopy face and pretended the bumping of Lucy's feet, now a pounding, was something far away. She concentrated on dinner. The stew was a sweeter version of the French bouillabaisse she remembered. She pried open the shells, pulling out tiny clams, and peeled the larger shrimp. "It's wonderful," she said to

Nani as she dunked the bread in the broth, "and the salad too. What's the chopped fruit?"

Nani smiled with pride. "Sweet pears from our garden last summer. I put them up with our pineapple and papaya. I've nearly a dozen jars left of each in the cold cellar."

The meal progressed, the father silently returning to his book, the grandmother pulling him out and toward the child, Meredith watching, and for a brief moment, forgetting herself.

"Mr. Fitzhugh," she began again, determined to capture his attention.

He glanced up and frowned. "Yes? And call me Henry. Fitzhugh sounds like my father."

"Tsk, tsk," Nani said under her breath, shaking her head, "and may he rest in peace."

Meredith used her most charming voice. "Henry, I won't impose on you any longer. How can I leave and no longer be a burden?"

"You fly," he said with obvious sarcasm.

Her heart pounded. "Fly? Isn't there a road?"

"The road goes to the airport and from there you fly. Maui is an island, remember?"

"Of course. It's an island." Could she get on a plane again? Surely a big jet wouldn't be a problem...but they sometimes crashed too.

Nani rested her rough hand on Meredith's arm. "Miss Campbell, please stay and heal. We want you to stay. We give you *me kealoha,* our warmest welcome. Hana-lani will heal you. It holds the suffering and the healing of many gone before."

"We want you to stay!" cried Lucy. She clapped her hands and her high-pitched scream once again sent tremors through Meredith's skull.

"Quiet, little one," Nani said to Lucy. "The pretty lady has a headache."

"Thank you," Meredith said to Nani, then looked at Lucy with distaste. She *had* to get her life back, get some kind of control. "Find a car then, and I'll drive to the airport. Or a taxi." *One step at a time,* she thought.

"God...," Henry began.

"Be praised," Nani whispered.

"Get the woman a car, Nani!" He glanced at Meredith with outright hostility. "Or drive her yourself. *I'll* drive her, if need be."

"When she's better," Nani said.

"And when will that be?" he growled.

"Soon, Henry, soon." She turned to Meredith. "Don't pay any mind to Henry. He's still grieving."

Meredith accepted the verdict and finished her stew in silence. She could use a few more days to heal, especially her face. It was remarkable bouillabaisse, and she was hungry. But what was up with this man? He was different from others she had known, and nearly as rude as the kid, maybe ruder. His wire-rims were lopsided, his clothes wrinkled, and he looked as though he hadn't slept in years. Did grief do that to someone? But he was alone now, it seemed.

Seven

The following morning, under a sky of puffy white clouds drifting to the sea, Meredith sat in a lounge chair on the back verandah and watched the chocolate lab follow Lucy toward the rolling surf. A white sunhat covered the child's curls, and she screeched in delight as the dog barked. Old Nani lumbered behind, swinging her arms wide to keep her balance. Lucy was running now, her thin brown arms bent like a racer, and Nani was screaming to slow down. The shepherd followed Lucy at a discreet pace, not wanting to leave Nani behind, but from Meredith's god-like perch on the verandah, she sensed he had an eye on Lucy too. Soon they turned into small specks, having reached the shore and the tide pools, Nani holding Lucy's hand, the dogs jumping from rock to rock and barking. Eli plunged into the sea, retrieved something, turned, and swam back.

Once Meredith had searched tide pools. She and her father had balanced bare feet on rough rock and peered under boulders to view mini-worlds of spider crabs and guppies, as cold saltwater swirled in and out, tickling their ankles. She wanted to collect the many ocean treasures, shells and smooth spotted pebbles, tiny fish darting in murky puddles, but he stopped her. "They belong here," he said. "Let's leave them. This is their home."

As Meredith watched Nani and Lucy from the verandah, she sensed they belonged here too. But Meredith stood outside their world, an alien creature fallen from the sky. Where did she belong? Where was home?

San Francisco, she supposed. *Maybe New York. Certainly not Paris.*

She looked back at the rambling house. Someone else's. The old woman said the house would heal her. What did she mean?

Meredith sighed, touching the bandage on her face. Would she be scarred? Each day the physical pain receded, but the future loomed large and threatening. Without her face, what did she have? This Henry Fitzhugh was totally unaffected by her presence, but could she blame him? Tent dresses and scars were not exactly attractive.

And what about Nick? She tried not to think that far ahead.

Her lost clothes, bought in that sudden shopping spree in San Francisco, were the old Meredith. Without them, who was she now? A damaged body in far too much cotton. Nani said she would find things for her to wear, but they wouldn't be *hers*, her choice. Clothing identified her, expressed her personality, her true center. No, more than that, more than her identity, clothes gave her dignity, forced others to see her as she wanted to be seen. How else would others know who she truly was deep inside, except by what she wore on her outside? Why, clothes were like a descriptive label, a book blurb, a biography in cloth. They were her signature, her fingerprint. More than mere outer cover, clothes *were* the man, or woman, as the old saying went. And her naked body? Without clothes she was vulnerable, like an animal. Clothes protected her from that vulnerability, from the leering disrespect of men. They gave her power too, for she could control their lust, control their animal nature, force their respect and admiration, allowing only as much lust and leering as she desired.

She didn't want to think about the clothes the old woman would find. Hana must have shops somewhere, at least a mini-mall. She would start with the hotel shops. And soon.

⌘ ⌘ ⌘

That afternoon, as she dozed in the bamboo bed, Meredith heard the distant sounds of cars braking on gravel. Doors slammed, feet thumped on the porch stairs, women and children giggled. She peeked through the curtains to the drive. Rusty jeeps and rattletrap Fords arrived and departed, leaving parcels, bags, and baskets on the front stoop.

Nani and Lucy carried the donations upstairs, and Meredith helped spread them on the bed: tees, shorts, and underwear, sizes four and six, wrapped in brown paper or Hasegawa plastic bags; date bread and taro rolls in plastic wrap; canned fruit in a brown grocery bag; giant papayas and tiny bananas in baskets; bottles of coconut rum and a six-pack of beer.

"I announced your arrival at church," Nani said, nodding happily, "and looky here."

"How long will this go on?"

Nani was sorting and handing food to Lucy to take to the kitchen. "Probably another day, then they'll leave us alone." She smiled her gummy grin. "Would you like to join us for tea in the library?"

"Sure." Why not? Maybe the mysterious Henry would be there.

"At four." Nani lumbered down the stairs, Lucy behind her.

⌘ ⌘ ⌘

"We have tea!" Lucy cried as she led Meredith into the shadowy room off the entry.

A cathedral ceiling angled over tall vertical windows covered by heavy draperies. The spacious room, Meredith thought, must once have been the living room. Today it seemed more like a library. Books lined the walls. Bamboo chairs grouped around a card table stacked with more books, papers, *Chutes and Ladders*, and *Beginning Scrabble*. Two wing chairs faced a low coffee table. The room smelled musty and the stale air pressed close.

Meredith walked to the windows and pulled aside a faded green panel.

The view was spectacular, much like the view from the back verandah, but from a higher point on the rise. Beyond the broad lawn, black-rock cliffs fell to a sapphire sea that swelled and rolled as though powerful hands pulled the waters from below. Tall fan palms waved in the trade winds, and, far to the right, loomed Haleakala. Charcoal clouds hovered about the mountain's peak as a ray of sun shot behind them. Sunset was early for Hana-lani under the mountain.

"A perfect place for a spa," Meredith whispered.

"Keep those closed," Nani said from behind her.

Meredith turned. "But it's so beautiful."

The old woman's hands rested defiantly on her hips, as though her authority was unquestioned. "He wants them closed, for his collection."

"His collection?" Meredith let the drapery fall into place.

"His books must not be exposed to the light."

"That's too bad." She sat in a wing chair and gazed into the gloom.

"I'll get the tea," Nani said as she turned toward the kitchen and began her shuffle across the room. "Eli and Alabar, come. Lucy, keep Meredith company. Be a proper hostess."

"But I want to help you," Lucy whined. She crawled into the other wing chair.

They sat in silence. The child, her brown legs swinging, watched Meredith. Meredith picked at her nails, dismayed by their long ragged edges and chipping paint. How she needed a manicure.

The filtered afternoon light was fading and she rose to peek once again between the draperies. The reflected sun had turned the cumulus strands a deep fuchsia. She sighed. Such beauty! How could they hide it? She turned quickly at the sound of footsteps.

Nani followed Henry, who carried a bottle of rum and a glass balanced on a book. He set them on the low table, settled in the chair opposite Lucy where Meredith had been sitting, and poured an inch into his glass. He opened his book and, between sips, twisted the ring on his finger as he read silently.

Nani turned to Meredith. "Miss Campbell? Would you like tea, or perhaps something stronger?" The old woman frowned at her grandson, but Henry ignored her.

Meredith looked at Henry's glass. Why not? She was off the heavy medications, and her cheek throbbed. She would switch to a different painkiller. "A vodka martini?" But she would please her hostess. "And tea, if it's all right."

"A martini?" Nani seemed perplexed.

"Just some vodka on some ice then?"

"We might have some." Nani pulled up two wicker chairs, offered one to Meredith, and turned to a bar off the library. She returned with a tumbler and set it carefully on the table. "I'll get the tea." She lumbered toward the kitchen.

"Cheers." Meredith raised her glass to Henry, but he seemed

oblivious to her presence. She sipped her drink and sighed as the cool liquid warmed her inside, and looked at Lucy who stared at her with her large brown eyes. Henry continued to read, his glasses slipping down his nose.

Nani returned and set down a tray. She peeked into the brown teapot and poured the steaming liquid into three mugs. She pointed to a small honey pot and a pitcher of milk, then sliced banana bread on a cutting board. Adding honey and a little milk to one of the mugs, she carefully handed the tea to Lucy, lowered herself into the fourth chair, spread her napkin on her wide lap, and nibbled a bit of bread.

Meredith watched them as she sipped her cocktail, then studied Henry. His silence challenged her. He seemed the quintessential mystery man. He wasn't bad looking for his age, with thick dark hair streaked with silver. His mustache and beard, coupled with his glasses, made him look distinguished, and his regular features held a boyishness that made him seem vulnerable, appealing. His shoulders were broad and his biceps visible under his short sleeves. A bit of dark chest hair teased her from the vee of his white shirt. He wore denim cutoffs and rubber sandals.

But why did he choose his old books over this spectacular view? She couldn't understand such a man. Fortunately, she didn't have to.

She reached for her tea, having finished her vodka. Things were looking up.

Suddenly Henry spoke into his rum. "So, Ms. Campbell, it seems we have the pleasure of your company a little longer."

"I'll find a room in town," Meredith purred. "I don't want to inconvenience you."

"No," Nani said, "we want you here, don't we, Henry?"

"The princess stays!" screamed Lucy.

Meredith's head pounded, and she groaned.

"You're from San Francisco, Ms. Campbell," Henry said.

"Yes."

"And what brought you to our remote island paradise?"

"I...heard about the hotel...the Hotel Hana, and...thought it would be a nice place to...you know, get away." Desperately, she sought a change of subject.

"I see. Alone? With a drug dealer?" He frowned. "And what did you do in San Francisco, if you don't mind my asking?"

He was judging her! "I...was in investment banking of sorts...."

This was going all wrong. *He* was taking the initiative.

"Oh?"

"I interviewed clients...and what about you?"

"So you were in finance?" he asked, pushing on.

"I guess so—"

"What firm?"

"Kirby and Calhoun."

He smiled as though he knew them. "It's a small world. And are you still with them?"

"I left—"

Nani leaned forward. "Do you like to read, Miss Campbell?"

"Sure...I guess so—"

"You guess a good deal, Ms. Campbell," Henry said, smirking.

"Please, call me Meredith." He was laughing at her!

Nani rested her hand on Meredith's arm. "Maybe you could read to Lucy."

Lucy jumped up. "Let the princess read to me!"

"She's way behind in her schooling, Henry," Nani added. She raised her finger to Lucy. "Softly, little one, softly. Remember your manners."

Henry ignored his grandmother and glanced at his wall of books. "Tell me, Meredith, what did you read last?"

"Why, I just finished the latest issue of *Vogue*." She paused, then realized more was expected. "And before that an excellent novel."

"A novel?" He looked genuinely interested.

"One by...let me see...I think it was Darryl Cole...or was it Cowan..."

He smiled as though possessing secret knowledge and tapped the arm of his chair. "The romance novelist Darryl Caroll? I should have guessed." He steepled his fingers as if another piece of a puzzle had been put in place.

"It was quite good, really. There was this Bavarian count who met a poor seamstress, but she didn't know he was a count and..."

"To be sure."

She rose from her chair. "Books aren't everything." She tossed her head, an effective gesture that spun her hair in all directions. "*Oh God,*" she said as she sat down carefully, holding her head.

"*Be praised,*" Nani breathed.

"I'm sorry," Henry said in a tone of sincere apology. "I've been terribly rude. You're still hurting. And you are our guest. As a matter of fact, you *could* be useful here. Someone needs to read to Lucy, and Nani cannot read." He glanced at his grandmother with a frustrated affection. "But she holds much wisdom in her head and heart."

Nani nodded and replaced Lucy's napkin, which had fallen on the floor. "In the old days few of our people could read. They believed words held *mana*, holy power. The Old Hawaiians kept such wisdom by speaking words only. They did not want to lose the power through writing." She sat back and clasped her hands on her lap.

Henry stared into the distance. "It's true. History and culture were transmitted from generation to generation orally. Literacy really began with Queen Kaahumanu. She invited the missionaries to teach her people, and she herself only learned toward the end of her life." He smiled to himself. "It's ironic, really, this bit about words having power. Today the written word is considered an intensification of power, a distillation even. Much the same, but today an *acceptable* tool to gain more power. In a way, the old Hawaiians were absolutely right."

Henry seemed to be carrying on a conversation with himself, Meredith thought.

Suddenly he turned to Meredith and studied her. She sipped her tea, a brew of herbs with hints of pineapple. She looked at the floor, enjoying his gaze, then up.

He gestured with his folded wire-rims and crossed one leg over another. "American missionaries were surprised when the natives recited entire books of the Bible."

She glanced at him. He was observing her as though she were a vessel he could fill with information.

Nani nodded vigorously. "It's true. Henry taught history, my Henry did." She beamed.

"Nani," Henry said, "also retains her learning in her head. But my daughter needs to read and write. Would you read to her while you are here, Miss Campbell? It would help. My work takes up so much of my time."

"Your work?"

"Then it's settled." Setting down his empty glass, he walked to the shelves. He located a worn copy of *Peter Pan* and handed it to her.

Meredith opened it. The pages were yellowing and the binding faded. James Barrie. This didn't look like the movie she remembered. Lucy waited, adjusting her headband and straightening her blouse, as though getting ready for a photograph.

Meredith began to protest, but Henry was gone.

Lucy squeezed into the chair with Meredith. "Will you teach me, Princess, please?"

Meredith frowned. "Sorry, I'm no teacher, and I've got to make a call."

"Tsk, tsk," whispered Nani, stacking the dishes on the tray.

Meredith disentangled herself from the child, set the book in Lucy's lap, and walked to the phone in the entry. Her rent was due today. She would touch base with Parker, give an edited version of her situation. No need to mention the crash.

The line was still dead.

"When will the phone be fixed?" she asked as she returned.

Nani didn't reply. She was rocking Lucy on her lap. The child, sucking her thumb, was curled against Nani's wide bosom.

Nani frowned and gently set Lucy on her feet. Holding the child's free hand, she led her toward the windows. She drew the drapes open a few inches and began to sway her hips. The last light had set the clouds on fire over a sea of silvery glass. She released Lucy's hand and began to move her own hands through the air, as though telling a story, up and down, her fingers weaving a poem, her soft soprano lilting through the room. *Aloha oe....*

Lucy copied her, thumping her tiny brown feet on the hardwood floor and laughing. She reached for Meredith's hand and pointed to the dusky sky with its pink ribbons. "*Ahiahi,*" she said.

"The edge of day and evening," Nani explained, "when the sun sets the *ao* on fire and *po* begins."

Meredith felt she was on the edge of a dream. "*Ahiahi.* You mean twilight, I suppose."

Eight

Having found a use for the girl—to read to his daughter—Henry Tennyson Fitzhugh fled to his study, dropped into his deep leather chair, and turned on his laptop. The walls were lined with more books, the ones he needed for his current project. He had arranged the reference works within arm's reach: thesauri, dictionaries, word menus. The *Oxford English Dictionary* filled a shelf of its own. The rest of the shelves held history with some poetry, theology, and philosophy. When Henry came home to Hana, he had brought all of his books, *their* books, over a hundred boxes flown in over six weeks, and he had no regrets. His books comforted him like few people could.

He opened the computer file on Maria's *Out of the Wasteland, a History of Ethics*, her working title.

This Meredith was a lightweight, another blond bombshell with little between the ears. Henry turned toward the cedar chest holding Maria's photo albums and lifted the lid. In the corner, nestled against the sweet-smelling wood, was his old baseball glove, worn and creased. He slipped it on his left hand. The leather was stiff, and he worked it with his fingers a bit, then punched the palm with his right fist. It still fit perfectly. He put it back and glanced at his pipe packed away in a shoebox with a half bag of stale Dunhill. His gaze rested for a moment on the shiny handle and moved quickly to the albums. Best to stay away from that habit. Nani didn't like it, and Lucy complained about his breath. A friend in Berkeley had died of throat cancer.

Henry chose a green leather-bound album with thick white pages. He recalled how Maria carefully inserted the pages, working the tiny screws onto steel posts to hold the book together. He turned the pages slowly and paused over an early picture, one that captured her zest, her love of life. Maria grinned, her thick dark hair, shoulder-length then, caught by the wind. She must have taken off her glasses, for her eyes were wide and had the myopic look of one who can't see clearly. He had chased her down the beach, called to her to turn, and snapped the shot. *Maria.* She knew how to pull him out of himself, make him laugh.

But she was also driven to succeed, as was he. To her it was a great game, the challenge of living, of going as far as you could and pushing farther. How he missed the *we*, the *us*, as though they were linked by an invisible string, a line that tugged him back to sanity when he strayed too far into work. They were true partners, at the university, in research, in everything. Their last project, the history of ethics in literature and letters, he would finish *for her.*

He recalled her excitement as she read T.S. Eliot, following the great poet's journey from despair to hope. She called it the "the re-awakening of the moral imagination," a rebirth of American culture, and she was going to midwife it singlehandedly, renew Western values herself, and speak for Eliot in this new twenty-first century. How could he not help her in such a quest? Their fields had dovetailed neatly, her English Lit and his Western Civ.

He walked to the window and looked out to the gray sea spread beneath the evening dusk. Why had he let her fly alone? Why had he thought his research so important? It could have waited. They had fought, and she had slammed the door behind her.

The laptop remained open on the desk, waiting. He turned to the screen.

He would complete what they had started. He would write the words here, in Maria's house, Hana-lani, where she had grown up with old Nani, the house where they had met, where he too had lived part of his youth, where the taro fields looked over the sea, fields long gone. He gazed outside, over the lawn, and saw his bride in her white dress, standing under the pagoda shaded by the hau tree.

All of Hana must have witnessed their wedding that day. Nani's pastor held the Bible, his robes blowing in the wind, as he waited alongside Henry. Then Maria approached. Her grandmother lifted the long lace veil above the wild grass and laid it down with a graceful bow. Nani had woven plumeria blossoms into Maria's dark braids and coiled them into a crown on her head. Now Henry recalled how time stood still, as though he was poised between two worlds, listening to a distant melody, piercingly sweet, his heart pounding in his ears. She was so beautiful he could barely speak, but he found her wide eyes behind the lace, and he was anchored, home. They exchanged rings with shaking fingers. A breeze rustled the trees, Maria's veil blew against her lips, and they promised to love forever, *till death us do part.*

And, twenty years later, all of Hana must have witnessed Maria's burial in the cemetery alongside the Congregational Church. On the flight home to Hana, he had gripped the enamel box holding her ashes, willing himself to become one with them. Nani insisted that her granddaughter be buried in the churchyard where her people rested, not in the fields as Henry would have preferred, and he had deferred to his elder, as the young must forever do, showing respect for their wisdom. Although Maria was not a believer either, she would have done the same.

There, under the hibiscus tree amidst the other graves, the villagers wailed a dirge mingling Old Hawaiian and Christian rituals, and Henry sprinkled the ashes into the rich earth, sprinkling part of himself—all of himself it seemed—on that gray day, to be buried with his wife. He shoveled the earth over the sooty matter and worked the soil with his bare feet. Tutu Nani joined him, dancing about the grave of her granddaughter, her hips swaying, her hands praying, sending her incantation to heaven.

"Ashes to ashes," the pastor had read as his white robes blew in the warm wet winds. "May her soul rest in peace."

Henry twisted his ring about his finger and blinked. The room was dark. He switched on the desk lamp and returned to the screen. Where had he left off?

Knowing that past and present really are one, Eliot draws upon the myths and the symbols of several cultures to find the questions that we moderns ought to ask. Myth is not falsehood; instead, it is the symbolic representation of reality. From ancient theological and poetical and historical sources, burningly relevant to our present private and public condition, we summon up the moral imagination.
— Russell Kirk

Burningly relevant?

Someone knocked. He ignored it. They knocked again. It soon became a steady pounding. He rose wearily. "What is it now?" he cried as he undid the latch.

She stood in the doorway, her blond hair falling in waves to her shoulders and shimmering in the lamplight. She wore a green tee and white shorts, frayed at the edges. Both articles of clothing appeared far too small.

She touched her bandaged face self-consciously. "It's Nani. Please come, Mr...er...Henry. She won't wake up."

"Probably another of her fainting spells." Henry sighed and followed the girl. Surely a false alarm.

Her shorts clung to her buttocks, and her legs were long and firm. He pulled his eyes away as heat rushed through his body, and he focused on his grandmother, stretched out on the verandah chaise. Lucy was brushing Nani's face with a red hibiscus blossom, whispering, "Wake up, Tutu Nani, wake up." The dogs whimpered.

Henry knelt, lifted her gray head onto his arm, and felt for a pulse. It was slow, but regular. Nani's eyes fluttered open.

"Let's get you into the house, Nani," Henry said as he helped her up. "You had one of your spells."

"So I did." She looked around and smiled. "So I did, but I'm right as rain now. No need to help me; I'm right as rain." She patted her long frizzy hair, arranging it.

Henry helped her down the hall to her room, where he laid out her nightgown. "Can you get into bed okay? Do you want something to eat or drink?"

"I'm fine, Henry, but Lucy hasn't had her dinner," she said hoarsely. "I must heat up something."

"I'll do it," Henry said. "You rest now, Nani." He backed out the door, closing it gently.

The blonde waited in the hall.

"She'll be fine. This happens occasionally." Henry turned toward the kitchen.

"Aren't you calling a doctor?"

"No need. Like I said, it happens, and she recovers. She won't want to see Sammy. She believes in natural remedies, holistic stuff...and prayer. I've never been able to make her see sense."

"What about Lucy? Shall I fix something to eat?"

Henry studied her. Her tone was genuine. She really wanted to help.

"Sure," he said with gratitude, "and something for yourself. I'm not hungry." He grabbed the bottle of rum and closed his study door behind him.

⌘ ⌘ ⌘

Someone was pounding on the door again. How long had he been staring at the Kirk quote? He probably should reread Eliot's *Four Quartets*. It had been difficult the first time through. He picked up the rum. The bottle was nearly empty.

"Go away!"

"Please, Henry..."

The blonde. He rose and unlatched the door, his anger rising.

She wore a thin muslin nightdress, one of Nani's, and carried a tray with a bowl of steaming soup. "Lucy's in bed—it's nearly ten. You really should eat something." She set the tray on the desk and glanced at the computer screen. "Are you a writer or something?"

"Or something." The soup smelled familiar, last night's stew without the fish. "What did you add?" He was suddenly ravenous.

"Leftover vegetables. And I fed the dogs. Are they okay outside all night?"

"Of course. This is Hawaii."

"What are you writing?" She sat down in a leather chair in the corner, his reading chair with the three-way lamp, her legs apart, her bare feet planted on the floor. He could see the faint outline of her body under the gown.

"You wouldn't understand."

"Try me." She leaned forward, her hands on her knees.

"Another time. Now if you will excuse me, Ms. Campbell."

"Call me Meredith," she said, standing up. "Say, what do you do for exercise? You know, keep in shape? Any workout machines? Weights? Stairmasters? Lifecycles?"

She's a spa woman. "We keep a full gym in the room next to the massage and steam rooms." He tried to keep a straight face.

"Cool! And where's that, might I ask? I need to get started. I've missed too much time already. One has to keep up with these things. I'll begin my program first thing in the morning. My leg is fine, nearly healed." She ran her hands along her hips, pulling the shift close to her body.

Henry stared and tried to refocus his attention on the conversation. How long had it been since he'd slept with a woman? "I'm sorry, we don't actually have a workout room here on the premises. We use the facilities at the hotel."

"Oh," she said, sounding disappointed. A light came into her eyes. They were cornflower blue. "Why, you were conning me."

"Just a little."

"You think you're so smart with all your books? Well, you can have them." She turned on her heel and tried to open the door, stopped by the automatic latch-lock. "You've got a regular barricade here."

He stepped behind her and reached around her shoulders to work the lock, inhaling the aroma of her hair. Jasmine, Maria's shampoo. His body ached, and he allowed his face to brush the thick waves. He pulled himself back.

She turned, her eyes gleaming with triumph. "Books aren't everything, Henry Dickens," she said, raising her brows, obviously pleased with her creativity. "You need to get out more, my boy." Her finger followed the vee of his shirt and circled in his chest hair.

Henry groaned and closed his eyes. "It's late, Ms. Campbell; you'd better go to bed. You barely know me, and you are far too young. *And* still recuperating."

"Of course, Professor. You know best." She spun on her heel and disappeared down the hall.

He returned to his desk, listening to the tap of her bare feet on the stairs and the faint creak of her door closing. His face burned. His heart raced.

He opened the slim volume of *Four Quartets.*

Time past and time future
What might have been and what has been
Point to one end, which is always present...

How he longed for Maria.

Nine

That night Henry dreamed of Maria. He woke at dawn in a cold sweat, his shorts soaked, as a pale light filtered through the shutters. Sitting on the edge of his cot, he rubbed his face hard, trying to hold onto the dream, but it was gone. He walked to the adjoining bath and threw cold water on his face.

He changed his clothes, laced his trainers, the routine steadying him, and stepped through the back door into the early morning. He loped toward the sea, the dogs soon close behind.

At the cliff's rim he followed a level trail high above the water. He had run this trail often as a boy, at first when no one knew, in dawn or dusk, and the motion of his legs never failed to smooth the rough edges of his mind. Living at Hana-lani in the last of his boyhood, on the border of adolescence, he had known urges he couldn't explain, and running calmed him. Books helped too, as they always did. But when he looked at Maria, her young body growing in remarkable ways, his urges surged, telling him to touch her hair, to stroke her smooth brown arms, to pull her close. He often fled in those early years, running along the trail by the sea. Later, when they were older, Maria ran with him.

As a boy, he would stop and look back at the house silhouetted against the mountain. When he ran in the dawn and glanced back, the first light coming up over the glassy waters would bathe the back of the house, revealing Hana-lani's peeling paint of a forgotten color, the gray-planked verandah, the sagging lounge chairs. When he ran in the dusk and paused to look back, the last rays behind Haleakala would strike the green, pitched roof and throw long shadows over the taro fields, down to the sea. The dormer windows would peer down upon him like a mother's eyes, and Henry held the old house close, as though it measured his heartbeat, keeping time to his life, straddling the mountain, the fields, and the sea. With Hana-lani at his back, he would resume his run.

When he had run with Maria they had run silently, for they were young and green and unhurried by their past. Time belonged to them, stretching ahead forever, and their matched pace filled them with peace. They would return to the sagging chaises and gulp pitchers of water with lemon slices. When he left for Cal Berkeley in the fall of '69, they promised to write, and they did, he more than she. Summers, bracketed by June and September, were precious, and she joined him in Berkeley three years later.

This early morning Henry jogged purposefully, a middle-aged man carrying the runs of many years and the sweat of his night dream. The dogs padded ahead and re-marked their territory, their tongues hanging and dripping, their paws sending out puffs of red dust.

He stopped and gazed over the glassy water undulating in the dawn. His heart beat hard. He wiped his brow, rested his hands on his hips, and leaned forward to catch his breath. The sun had risen but remained behind scattered clouds of silvery gray, the ocean a steely slate. The calm of the sea at daybreak affected him powerfully, a soothing drug, and he sighed. But his heart continued to pound. He rested on a flat rock as the dogs drank from a nearby stream.

With the house behind him like an ancient angel owning his memory, Henry stared at the smooth waters.

His college years in Berkeley were war years, and he joined the Vietnam protests, marching, waging sit-ins with the righteous knowledge of how things should be. Surely, they believed, they were the first generation to oppose war, to proclaim peace; surely they would show others that peace was good, war was bad.

How simple they had been, Henry now thought, to preach their ideals as though they alone owned them, as though they were the chosen few, the elite, who could enlighten a sick society. How proud, how unbelievably arrogant, they had been.

But the times drew them close in spite of their muddled thinking—or perhaps because of it. He and she and their friends, bound by the thick glue of self-congratulation, of intended if unrealized sacrifice, sat in circles and shared weed and beer and cheap wine. They told stories, laughing cynically at their materialistic elders, elders who paid their tuition. One friend cut off a finger to avoid the war, another blinded himself, another forged psychiatric papers. Some fled to Canada. Some were arrested and indicted, welcoming, in their innocent ignorance, jail. All of them covered their fear with ideals of peace, for most were simply scared to death of going to war, terrified of dying or being maimed.

Even now, gazing out to sea, Henry felt that fear.

And some of the brave, or those caught with no creative dodges, enlisted, like his cousins Jeff and Derek, drafted in the lottery, having unlucky birthdays. Some returned whole; some returned damaged in soul or body; some didn't return. Henry's cousins lay beneath foreign soil with no markers, their deaths fueling the peace movement. Henry squeaked by with college deferments.

Henry and Maria marched those years side by side, one cause replacing another, through school, through teaching, through doctorates. They had agreed on so many things back then. It wasn't until the terrorists hit the twin towers on September 11, 2001 that things changed.

Now Henry held his wrist, checking his pulse. He called the dogs and resumed his run, hoping to bury his aching regret in action. They had fought often the months before she died, fought over Iraq and the new world in which they found themselves. The devastation in New York, broadcast into their home as Lucy played, horrified Henry. He had looked up from his books and saw the planes head for the towers, the explosions, the billowing black smoke, the screams, the stunned reporters searching for words. Over and over the news replayed, a repeating nightmare. But it was no nightmare. It was real.

The sun was up now, above the clouds, and sweat dripped between his shoulder blades, soaking his shirt. He drank from his water bottle and headed back.

Hana-lani rose on his left and he held the house in his sightline, his mind filled with the past. Maria had kept her anti-war stance. But he had balked.

"We were attacked," he said. "We were attacked by a foreign power on our own soil. We have to protect ourselves. We have to protect Lucy."

"No," she said. "They are people who hate America, and hate for good reason. Look at Hollywood. Look at the Internet."

The debate raged and finally drifted into resentful silence, a silence that wedged them apart like never before.

Five months later, her plane fell into San Francisco Bay. Mechanical failure, they said.

Approaching the house, he slowed to a walk, allowing his body to cool down. Nani sat on the verandah chaise with a mug of tea.

She frowned. "Been looking for you. You worry me, Henry."

"Went for a run, Nani."

She handed him a towel. He wiped himself down and sat beside her.

She patted his leg. "Sammy's been phoning."

"About the girl?" He glanced sideways at his grandmother.

"Wants to see *you*, Henry."

"Why?"

"Does he have to have a reason to see his hero? He doesn't understand why you avoid him."

"I don't see anyone, Nani. It's not him. I'm not ready, that's all."

"He doesn't understand."

"He's a boy. Explain it to him."

"He's thirty-five, Henry."

"Always seemed like a boy to me."

"Followed you around like a puppy dog when you came home from California in the summertime."

Henry laughed and it felt good. Maybe he should see Sam, spend some time with him. Take him fishing. He recalled his surprise when Samuel Tagami from Hana appeared in his history class. The young man, so earnest, had been one of his top students, and Henry had been impressed. He and Maria cooked for him on weekends in their shingled cottage on Hillegass Avenue, and the three of them discussed philosophy into the night. A good lad, bright and promising. Sammy hadn't disappointed his admirers, or his family, or those who helped pay for his education. Going straight through in four years and transferring to medical school was pretty good for a country boy.

But it had seemed a waste to Henry that he had chosen to

specialize in family medicine and a waste when he set up practice in Kahului. He gave away most of his time, and talent, and what was left he gave to the Hana Clinic. When he was paid, it was most likely in produce. It was a good thing he didn't have a family to support and lived with cousins.

"You shouldn't treat him poorly, Henry."

"I'll call him, Tutu." Henry stood and leaned on the railing. The paint was peeling, and he scraped a bit with his fingernail, watching the dust fall onto the ti plants below.

"Did Sam know about Lucy?" Nani asked, her voice strained.

Henry heard the words but didn't turn. "Know what about Lucy?"

"Her birth, her hearing problem? Did you tell others, Henry, and not tell me?"

He didn't want to see her questioning eyes but forced himself to turn and face her. He could never hide from Tutu Nani for long, and he had known this moment would come.

"I'm sorry, Nani. Maria didn't want you to know. Anyway, Lucy wasn't actually *deaf*. We hoped we could fix it."

She nodded forgivingly. "And you did, Henry, you did fix it."

Henry sat next to her in the chaise, leaning toward her, relieved to confess. He hated keeping things from Nani. "But we should have been honest with you."

Nani waited.

Henry tried to explain. "Maria was afraid, afraid you would say she was to blame. She blamed herself."

"I see."

Maria's tears in the hospital had bewildered Henry. She didn't want to live. She didn't want to see Lucy. She was convinced that, at forty-three, her age and health had caused the baby's hearing loss. It was postpartum depression with an added twist, the doctor said. Henry had taken paternity leave that semester to nurse both daughter and wife.

"And," he added, "in answer to your question, Sammy knew. He was around in those days. He helped a lot."

As Tutu Nani wrapped her arms around him, his muscles relaxed, and for the moment, he was twelve again.

Ten

Days passed, and Meredith fell into a routine of reading to the child in the morning and watching her in the afternoon while Nani napped. Henry appeared at dinner, and since that evening in his study, had retreated farther and farther away. He addressed all remarks, what little he said, to either Nani, Lucy, or his food and drink, and returned to his cave.

Meredith was both perplexed and excited by the challenge. Rarely had she known a man to turn her down. Some had put her off for a time, but none, in the end, had refused. There was this mishap with Nick and his wife, but she was sure his recent indiscretion was merely a temporary lapse in judgment. Her goals remained the same: to allow him back when he begged appropriately and in the meantime to repair the damage to her face. If she could bear the quiet and the boredom, she would stay on here a bit longer. It would be worth it. Staying in a hotel would bankrupt her. She didn't know when she would look good enough to return to San Francisco, and Hana-lani wasn't half-bad as a convalescent home. Hopefully the scars would be minimal when covered by makeup. The headaches were receding.

The thought of flying terrified her. That, too, could wait. She dreamed she was falling through the sky, her stomach lurching. When would it end?

She studied her face daily in the mirror and noticed significant progress. She peeled off the old bandages carefully, wincing at the sting, imagining a sudden hemorrhage. Doctor Sammy had left antibiotic ointment to smooth over the jagged lines of the gashes, and she reapplied the wide adhesive strips over the salve, patting the edges gently. Her thigh cut, more of a puncture than a tear, was nearly healed, and Sammy said that once the danger of infection was over, it would be fine. It was still an angry red, but she trusted him, and appreciated his regular visits. She reapplied the bandage there too.

She checked her hips for bulges and imagined her widening waistline, considering her high-carb diet and little exercise. She did stretches, lunges, and abdominal crunches on the grass matting in her room. She searched for a scale.

One afternoon, as Nani and Lucy napped, she roamed the house, looking for a TV, wondering what had happened in *Sex in the City*. She would settle for anything producing rhythm and speech—TV, radio, CD player—but found nothing. She stumbled over a ukulele leaning against a wall near the back door, recalled distant strumming late at night, and righted it carefully. The floors creaked as she tiptoed in her bare feet, scanning tables, looking in desks, pulling out drawers. No magazines. No newspapers. Nothing.

Henry's books in the dim library seemed unpromising. Still, she pulled a few down. The yellow pages smelled musty; the type was of another time, the words strange. Milton and Shakespeare, Joyce and Yeats, Johnson and Pepys. An entire row of Britannicas. Durant and Boorstin. Locke, Rousseau, Hume. The names rang bells with no tune, distant notes from far away. She found a slim volume of Jane Austen, recalling the movie *Pride and Prejudice* with that cute Colin Firth, and read the first page hopefully...but quickly closed it. Not much action there, nothing to really grab her. The shelves reminded her of forced study hall in her high school library, the righteous rows of books watching her like prison guards, accusing her of not measuring up. She felt trapped and inadequate just looking at them.

In the kitchen, cluttered with appliances, utensils, cutting boards, bowls and platters, forgotten foods from dinner, she found a wall calendar on the pantry door. In the squares someone had neatly printed the events: dancing/hotel, Sammy, Quilting Club, Prayer Group, Seniors. There were birthdays. A funeral was crossed off from weeks ago. Meredith lifted February's page and found babies due in March. *Lucy* was written in a child's scrawl on Easter Sunday, April 11, and under it in neat script, *Baptism*. Five weddings were scheduled for Saturdays in May and June.

"Looking for something?"

Startled, Meredith turned.

Nani stood in the kitchen doorway, her fists on her hips.

Meredith smiled nervously. "Just curious. Sorry, didn't mean to pry."

"Snooping around?" Nani's eyes narrowed.

"God..."

"Be praised."

"Really, just passing the time."

"Come and sit and have some iced tea."

Nani pulled out a stool for Meredith, then opened the refrigerator. She found a tall pitcher of tea and a bowl of lemon wedges. She pulled down two glasses from a shelf.

Meredith sat obediently, feeling a twinge of guilt. *A person has to do something around here,* she thought. *No need for her to get all huffy.*

Nani sat too. They stirred sugar into the amber liquid and squeezed the lemons. Nani's eyes were on her, and Meredith kept hers fixed on the tea.

"Now, Miss Meredith, don't you worry, you going to be okay. Just have a little patience, a little patience."

Meredith looked up to the crinkled brown eyes that tried to ease her restlessness. "Thanks," she said weakly.

"You saw my calendar? Henry helps me with the writing part. I can sound out some of it."

"You have many things planned."

"My *ohana*, my family, are many souls. Lou and I had seven children, and they had children, and then they had children. And so forth. You know how it goes." She laughed a large laugh and clapped her hands. Suddenly her face grew solemn. "Or do you?"

"Not really." Was she going to preach to her?

"Did you see my photo wall?"

"No." Meredith had almost finished the tea. Soon she could go.

"Come. I'll show you."

Nani set down her glass and led Meredith to the laundry room off the kitchen. Above the washer and dryer, photographs papered the wall, tacked with pushpins, layer upon layer. The old woman pointed to a black-and-white framed picture in the center of the huge collage. A man with a dark weathered face, ruggedly handsome, stood next to a beautiful island girl, her hair down to her waist. The girl wore a long cream satin dress.

"That's me and Lou," she said with pride as she took it down.

Meredith studied the portrait. It was like an old tintype, the couple standing formal and stiff. There was no question they were a handsome pair, and though they didn't smile, as was the fashion in those days, Meredith sensed an anticipated happiness.

"Our wedding day."

"Wow," Meredith said. "That's so sweet. He's handsome. And you...you're beautiful, Nani."

"Thank you, dear. But my Lou, my-oh-my, he was such a catch that I can never tell you how I loved him so! All the girls were after my Lou." She giggled a little.

Meredith smiled and pointed to the wall of photos. "And all these others?"

"We made most of them!" Nani chuckled and sat down on a stool in the corner.

"And Lou?"

Nani shook her head. "I had many good years with him. Not all peaceful, mind you—there were some rough patches—but we made it through with God's help. Then I lost him, twenty years ago now, when he sailed with the fishermen. He was too old, he knew that, but he went anyway. He was like that, never missing a chance, never turning anyone down. The storm came up suddenly. But then, they usually do."

"I'm sorry." Meredith wished she hadn't asked.

"But, Miss Meredith, I have memories of Lou that I shall hold close until I be with him in heaven."

"Of course."

Nani rose, the picture in her hand, and shuffled back to the kitchen. Meredith followed.

"Please sit with me a bit more," Nani ordered gently. "I feel like talking about him, and I need someone to listen."

Nani held the frame between her thick fingers and touched her husband's face, behind the glass. Meredith sat down and watched her, pulled into the woman's memory, entranced.

"I remember how we'd finish each other's sentences, we was that close. He knew what I was to say. and I knew what he was to say. Isn't that something?"

"It is."

"That doesn't mean we didn't have times when something big stood between us, something ugly and hateful, like a wild pig."

"Of course."

"But you know, little one, even those times, we'd snuggle together, and somehow our bodies would speak when our hearts couldn't. Now isn't that strange?"

Meredith thought about it. "It's strange but nice."

"It *was* nice." Nani grinned. "And that's how it was, Lou and me. Our bodies carried us through the rough waters good enough so we could sail again in the smooth. And it's nice now to remember that."

Meredith stood and kissed her on the forehead. "Thanks, Nani, thanks. That's sweet. Can I help you with dinner?"

⌘⌘⌘

Days passed, and Meredith was often left alone with the broken silence of the house. Nani tapped the floors as she slowly cleaned, humming and singing softly. Lucy screeched and padded through the rooms.

Each day Meredith checked her wounds, reapplying the bandages and assessing her progress. A little more time. Each day she wondered if she could board a plane. A little more time.

Family members dropped by on their way home from work, boys with scars and bandanas who worked in the yard, heavy girls with bags of groceries and cleaning buckets. They ran lawn mowers and piled clothes into the washer, pushing buttons and setting timers. "My *ohana*," Nani said, "my good children."

Meredith deduced that Lucy's loud and sometimes erratic voice was connected to her hearing loss. Perhaps that was why she wasn't in school. Didn't six-year-olds go to school? As she read to the child, sitting on the lawn on dry days and the verandah on wet ones, occasionally inside, in the dim library, she taught Lucy not to screech, to say "Oh" and "Cool" and "Wow" in little teeny tiny whispers.

"Come to my room, Princess," Lucy said on Monday morning, two weeks after the crash.

Lucy led her down the hall past Henry's office to an enclosed sun porch. Through the square windowpanes a flower garden could be seen, and today the rain fell gently on the leaves, straight and steady. A low table and chairs stood against the window. In the corner, stuffed animals and a Raggedy Ann sat on a cot with a pink quilt. White paper, colored paper, paint boxes, and crayons in mugs lined low shelves.

Meredith pointed to the wall above the shelves, papered with colorful drawings. "Did you paint all of these, Lucy?"

"I did," she whispered. "Cool!"

"They're amazing."

The colors were bold, and she recognized the subjects—sunsets, flowers, the front door of the house with its bell and cascading trellis vines. The brilliant hues reminded her of the swatches of fabric her mother set out when she prepared for a fashion show.

"Is this your father?" Meredith pointed to a stick drawing of a man.

Lucy nodded. "That's Papa."

His wire-rimmed glasses dwarfed his face, and something hung from his mouth. A pipe? Books filled the background. Meredith laughed.

"He doesn't like it," Lucy said. "He wants to stop smoking."

"I like it."

"You do?"

"I do."

"Want to keep it? I give it to you, a present."

"Really? Thanks." How could she say no?

Meredith peeled the tape and pulled the picture from the wall.

"And who are these other people?"

Lucy pointed to a small figure and a large figure, each wearing a triangular tent dress. "Nani and me."

"And what are you doing?"

"We're dancing."

"Like at twilight?"

She nodded. "Want to dance with us sometime?"

72

"I don't know, Lucy." When had she last danced?

"Please, come dance with us?"

"Where?"

Lucy placed her hands on her hips and tapped her toe. "At the hotel."

"We'll see."

"Will you come see me dance?"

"Sure." She would make an excuse later.

"Promise?"

Meredith hesitated, but the word slipped out. "Promise."

"Want to paint with me?"

"Why not?" Maybe the activity would quiet the child.

Lucy spread a plastic sheet on the table and arranged the paper and color pots. Meredith brought glasses of water from the kitchen, and Lucy laid out brushes next to the pots. They painted, dipping the brushes in the color, sliding them over the paper, and swishing them clean in the water. Meredith drew a picture of one of the windows in the room, the panes framed by the outside leaves and the sill holding tiny shells lined in a row, while Lucy chattered and painted too.

"Nani says time is love."

"Why is that, Lucy?"

"She says we need to paint together all the time."

"Paint together?" The old woman was full of riddles.

Once Meredith had painted like this, in Brooklyn long ago. The watercolor set held only a few pads of pigment in a long metal box. Her father gave the set to her for Christmas....

"Daddy, Daddy!" she cried when she opened the front door.

He swooped her into the air and set her down. A back door slammed, and a car gunned as it sped away. *Mommy.*

She was seven, and it was Christmas morning when she and her father had painted on newsprint spread beneath the tree. Her older brother watched TV in the den. She didn't see her father for quite some time afterwards, and in the years that followed, she tried to conjure his face from that Christmas, but the image soon blurred.

"He has other children, now," her mother said. "He has no time for us."

No time for me, Meredith thought, even to paint a silly picture....

"Do you like my picture?" Lucy whispered as she poked Meredith's arm with the end of a brush.

"It's cool."

"Cool." Lucy grinned.

The child had painted green grass and blue sea and a yellow sun above a mountain. Meredith pointed to a black patch in the corner. "What's that?"

"A cow."

"Right, I see it now."

"Nani says it's important to paint our love."

"Paint our love?"

"Like God did, when he made us."

Meredith nodded, watching Lucy as she bent over her work, dabbing on more cows, her face close to the paper. The dogs had curled near Meredith's feet, and a paw had found her toes. It was nearly lunchtime, and she wondered what Henry was doing. They made an unusual group, Meredith thought, as she recalled her evenings at Buzz's, Parker's parties, swizzle sticks and glances from the bar, cologne dabbed in her cleavage and behind her knees, the excitement of the hunt, of conquest. How soon could she go back? She touched her face. The pain and sensitivity were nearly gone. She should at least book a flight. But could she fly?

"I'm showing Papa," Lucy announced. Carefully, her palms flat and balanced beneath the wet paper, she carried the picture out of the room.

Meredith walked to the phone in the entry, finally got a dial tone, and checked her messages. Her gynecologist's office said she had missed her appointment and would be billed accordingly, her hair salon said the same, and there was nothing from Nick. Something must have happened to her message machine.

She dialed Parker. "Any news from Nick?" she asked as she stared outside at a sudden downpour. The rain hit the red earth and quickly pooled. "I've had trouble getting through."

"Nada, kid, nada. I let him know where you were, or where I thought you might be. Where *have* you been? Where *are* you?"

"Sorry, it's a long story."

"I checked your apartment and Nick's moved out, looks to me. I paid your rent too, thank you very much, and brought in the mail. Say, there's a letter from Florida. Isn't that where your dad is?"

"You'd better open it."

She heard the sound of paper tearing. "It's from the rest home."

"And?"

"It's a bill."

"You're kidding."

"Guess they tracked you down."

Where were all the wives and children now?

"Do they say anything about his condition?"

"Just a sec." Rustling paper. "Here's a note from the nurse. She says he's off the ventilator and stable, but not walking yet. Looks like they want to discharge him."

That's all I need. "I'll deal with it when I get back."

"Sure. Meredith, like where are you? You've been gone over two weeks."

Meredith sighed. "Like I said, it's a long story, but I made it to Hana and plan to stay a few more days before going to Wailea." That would explain her extended absence. The ingenuity of it pleased her.

"Why? Your tan not good enough?"

"It rains here, Parker. It rains a lot."

"I suppose it *is* their rainy season. But why Wailea?"

"It's sunny there, Parker. I need sun to tan." She stared at the rain pelting the garden.

"Ha, ha."

"Will you keep things together for me until next week?"

"Sure, kid, and I'll try to find out what's with Nick. Temporary insanity, probably."

As Meredith set the handset into its cradle, she considered dialing the airlines. She would face her fears. But then there was Lucy's dance.

She'd book the flight later.

Eleven

Each morning after reading a story, Meredith followed Lucy upstairs. Sitting on the bed, the child combed Meredith's hair, arranging it, keeping her hands clear of the bandages, as Meredith held up the mirror. Lucy's touch was gentle and sweet, and Meredith found herself falling into a trance during these moments, as though her head was being tickled by an angel. On Wednesday Lucy braided it into a single braid that fell down her back, and Meredith giggled when she looked at her image. She was Anne of Green Gables or Florence Nightingale. Thursday Lucy wound the hair on the top of her head, and, squealing in delight, let it freefall down.

Each day Meredith promised herself to call the airlines, and each day she postponed the call.

Friday Lucy pulled the comb through the thick strands and ran her tiny hands down the sides, patting the hair neatly. She jumped off the bed and looked up at Meredith seriously. "You need a pretty dress to go to the dance." She turned and opened the closet door, reached for a sheath of coral silk, and yanked it off a bent wire hanger. She laid it on the bed and looked expectantly at Meredith with her brown eyes.

"The dance? And when is that?" Meredith touched Lucy's headband, ran her fingers through her curls, and watched them bounce back into place. She had a doll with hair like that once, a real baby doll with eyes that blinked, and she dressed her in little sleepers her mother made. She traced the embroidery on Lucy's dress along the scalloped neck edge. The threads must have once formed a flower pattern, she thought. The faded purple and green meandered like a forgotten memory across the white cotton.

"Tonight."

"Where?"

"At the hotel."

"The Hotel Hana?" Meredith's memories of the hotel were not pleasant. She touched her two bandages. The stitches had dissolved as Sammy predicted. But could she go out in public? She thought not. It wasn't even three weeks since the crash.

Lucy handed her the dress, crumpled in her tiny hand. "Pleeeeze...come."

"It's lovely." Meredith held up the sheath, letting the shiny fabric fall straight. Looked to be a size four, if that.

"Aunt Maggie wore it before the baby. It's pretty. It's cool. Try it on."

Meredith slipped out of her tee and shorts and stepped into the silk. It clung to her skin, feather-light, smooth. She walked to the bath and looked in the mirror. It was tight enough, low-cut enough, and short enough. It showed off her shoulders too. It would do.

"You look pretty," Lucy said. "I'm telling Papa." She ran down the stairs.

Papa? Henry was coming? Perhaps the evening would provide another shot at Mr. Melancholy. Meredith found a small bottle of plumeria essence in the cabinet and dabbed some behind her ears. Not bad, she thought, leaning toward her reflection. She added a little makeup. Her afternoons in the backyard had helped her tan, and she sensed her reading to Lucy had scored points with the child's father. Her headaches were minimal. She would call the airlines immediately after the dance.

It was a real dress. She couldn't recall the last time she had worn a real dress.

⌘ ⌘ ⌘

The downpour didn't bother Tutu Nani-lei as they drove up to the hotel, packed into their old VW van, Nani in the front, Lucy and Meredith in the back, Henry driving. Nani waited for Henry to open her door, grabbed Henry's hand, pulled herself out, and led her entourage through the lobby to the dining room and a front-row table.

The restaurant expanded onto an outdoor verandah overlooking

Hana Bay, but tonight, with the steady rain, the folding glass doors were closed. The room was filling up. Tables of four angled toward a stage, and servers moved quickly along the polished wood floor, delivering drinks. Streamers hung from open beams and potted palms divided the audience from the backstage where the dancers gathered. A low hum of conversation carried anticipated pleasure as tourists, family members, and locals helped themselves to the buffet.

Henry ordered a double whisky, Meredith a martini. Nani ordered milk for Lucy, content with water for herself.

Nani took Lucy's hand and led her to the long bar of assorted dishes. She filled the child's plate with fern shoot salad, shredded luau pork, teriyaki chicken, lomi-lomi salmon, and Molokai purple potatoes. She ladled a bowl of chowder for herself. Returning to the table, she and Lucy ate quickly, excused themselves, and joined the dancers backstage.

Nani looked over her troupe. They seemed to be all there, except for Bill, who had the flu. Bill's sixteen-year-old daughter Kimberly smiled and Nani approached her. Kim's slim figure and thick dark hair reminded Nani of her own Lizzie, who, at fifteen, gave birth to Maria. Lizzie was the child she could not control, the girl that slipped out of her reach, the woman who would not, could not, listen. Every family had one, or two, she often thought, but that didn't help the hurt. She arranged Kim's puka shell necklace and kissed her cheek in blessing.

The dancing always brought Lizzie into her mind, and with Lizzie, the familiar sadness. What should, could, she have done differently? She had asked the Good Lord that question so many times there in the church's whitewashed sanctuary, staring at the giant wooden cross, that God was most likely pretty tired of hearing it. When the postman read to Nani her daughter's last letter with its New Zealand stamps, Nani knew despair darkened the words. *Dear sweet Jesus, I've lost her again,* Nani had thought. And she had raised Lizzie's little girl, Maria, as best she could, and was happy to do it.

"How's your papa?" Nani asked Kim. How like Lizzie she was, with the large dark eyes. But, unlike Lizzie, Kim seemed to like Hana.

"Crotchety, but he'll be okay." She wound her finger around her necklace.

"A nasty virus going around. We'll pray for him on Sunday."

"I won't tell him. He won't like it." She tossed her head and grinned.

"That's fine."

"But...I just want to say, Tutu Nani, thank you, thank you for asking." Her eyes held the hope of the young that the old might have answers. She had not yet been taught differently.

There were twenty-three dancers, ages six through ninety, and Tutu Nani-lei took her place, front row center. As their leader, she would bark commands that would move the dance forward and back, from one picture to another, from one story to another. Sharing the front row were the younger children, Lucy and nine others from Hana Elementary. Nani arranged the five teenagers in the second row and motioned for the women to stand behind them with the men in the back. The faces were every shade of brown and white, for several *haoles* had made the dance their own, and the bodies of every shape and size, spindly girls and lithesome teens, women heavy from childbearing and men lean from labor. The women wore green ti-leaf skirts, white blouses, and coral bracelets on their feet and arms. Triple strands of puka shells swung from their necks. The men wore white shirts and leafy leis.

Nani leaned back, checked her troupe, and nodded to a pair of musicians to the right. Nani's cousin Nellie sang the melody as she plinked a ukulele. Nellie's nephew Joe crooned the descant, keeping time on the drums. Their voices paired, soaring and weaving through the air.

The dancers began to dance. Their arms spread wide in offering, and their hips swayed gently. Their hands opened and closed, palms touching, separating, arcing, as they gestured to the people to draw near. Their fingers reached to the heavens, patted their hearts, pointed to the earth, and waved to the watchers, pulling all of these—the gods, themselves, the people, and the earth that bore them all—together, connecting heart and heaven, man and earth.

Old Nani-lei, with Lucy beside her, danced too, pulling the strands of their lives together, giving a melody to the disparate notes, harnessing, shaping, them, into a tune, making sense, if only for this moment, of their world. Somehow, the feet that tenderly tapped the floor, the hands that reverently stroked the heavens, the smiles that rode the trade winds, the hips that swung their welcome, all of these things, so central to human yearnings, Nani danced. Her dance celebrated the union of male and female, of parent and child, of play and work, unions reflecting heaven, and for Nani, embodying her God on earth.

Nani knew she carried the past into this room of watchers and listeners, the past of her people. As she danced, and the rhythm of the drums filled her dry bones, she reached back to her ancestors and pulled them into the present, offering them to the watchers before her, drawing them together with her heart.

And as she danced, she watched Henry with Meredith. She prayed her grandson would be healed by this woman who had come to them from the skies.

⌘ ⌘ ⌘

"It's lovely." Meredith applauded as the dancers filed out for a break. It wasn't reggae and it wasn't rock, but it was a welcome change from silence. They had filled their plates, he with roast pork and potatoes, she with chicken and salad. They had progressed from cocktails to a bottle of wine.

Henry stared into his chardonnay. "Yes."

"Do you dance too, Henry?" She leaned toward him and looked into his eyes, letting her breasts show to full advantage.

"Me? I'm afraid not." He glanced away, his cheeks flushed.

"What do you do for fun, Henry?" She brushed her finger along his arm.

"I like to read." He pulled his arm away and shifted in his chair, touching his ring.

"And what do you read, Henry?" She could play his game. She could follow his lead. Men could never resist that.

"History mostly, but lately, some poetry."

"Poetry?"

"Do you read poetry, Miss Campbell?" He glanced at her, then slipped his fork into the mashed potatoes.

She tried to think of a poet. "Why sure...let's see..."

He smiled slightly. He clearly didn't believe her. He looked her in the eyes as though suddenly on attack. "You can be honest, Miss Campbell. Please, I'd rather you be honest. You can't think of one poet, right?" He sounded amused.

She would try the innocent gambit. Maybe that would work. Her Eliza Doolittle to his Henry Higgins. "No, I'm afraid I can't." She lowered her lashes as though embarrassed, even ashamed. "I'm afraid I know nothing about poetry. Maybe you could teach me?"

"Somehow, I don't think so," he said as though he knew her better than she knew herself.

He's so arrogant, she thought. "What are you reading now?"

"Four Quartets."

"Poetry or music?" Had she missed a shift in topic?

"Four Quartets by T. S. Eliot."

"Who?"

"Thomas Stearns Eliot, probably the most important poet of the twentieth century."

"Oh, right, of course. Eliot." This was getting real close to boring, and she looked up to find Lucy as the dancers resumed their places. But she'd make one last foray before she drowned in this man's pride.

"Henry...," she began.

"Yes?"

"Why don't you give me something to read while I'm here, something important. You taught history?"

He nodded. "Western Civilization. European History, the Greeks and the Romans, for the most part."

Meredith recalled that Western Civ had been an elective in her college curriculum. She had taken Women's Studies instead. "Then you might have a beginners guide?"

He laughed, and Meredith sensed a truce.

"Sure, I've got just the book," he said. "It was on the freshman reading list. It's short, informative, and even poetic. In fact, your doctor wrote an excellent paper on it, as I recall."

"I'll look forward to it. My doctor? Sammy?" She sipped her wine.

"Sammy was one of my students, years ago."

Meredith wondered just how old this man was.

"When was that?"

"Let's see, that would be the fall of '89. Sammy was a freshman. A little wet behind the ears, a bit of a country boy, but sharp as a tack. Still is sharp, though you'd never know it with his easygoing manner."

Doctor Sammy must be close to her own age. "Why did he become a doctor if he did so well in history?"

"He didn't plan on it. He loved history, was one of my best students. But something happened that changed his mind."

"What was that? Too personal to tell?" Sammy was beginning to intrigue her. She wondered if he was married. *He* earned a living, had a real job. She wondered how Henry earned his.

"His sister died of leukemia."

"How terrible for him. Was she young?"

"Eighteen."

Meredith sighed. That was young, all right. "What is it? And why are you looking at me that way?"

"She looked a lot like you."

"You're kidding." The sister was Asian and looked like her?

"She was adopted. They were close. She followed him everywhere in Hana—to his ball games, on the fishing boat. He never sent her home, always included her."

"So he switched his degree to medicine?"

"He wanted to find a cure."

"But he's not in research now, is he?"

"One thing led to another. He got interested in stem cell therapy, and that led to bioethics, and finally, one day he chucked it all and became a family practitioner, joined an internal medicine group in Kahului." Henry reached for the wine and refilled their glasses. "Most of us were amazed. He had a promising research career. I think he had ethical doubts, and he's the kind of man who couldn't live with them." He looked at her seriously. "Some people are like that. Some aren't."

"And the Hana Clinic?" Meredith sipped her wine, not sure what he meant about ethical doubts. Couldn't stem cell research be totally good? Didn't everyone want to cure disease? Why, there was a TV show last month about that very thing....

"He donates his time. He gives back, as he likes to say. Sammy's a good man."

Meredith wondered why Sam chose to work in Hana when he could write his own ticket in any big city.

"Not what you would do?" Henry smiled his half-smile, seeming to read her mind.

"I don't think so." As soon as she said the words, Meredith regretted her tone.

With a look of mild frustration, Henry shook his head, then waved at Lucy.

Meredith sensed she lost something halfway through the conversation, as though he assumed she knew things she didn't. Was he laughing at her? She envied him, but she wasn't sure why.

"I'll find that book for you," Henry said as he signaled the server for the check.

Twelve

Saturday morning Henry found a tattered copy of Thomas Cahill's *How the Irish Saved Civilization*. He hoped it would bribe the girl to leave him alone.

He had mapped out his work on Maria's book (finish the research, outline the chapters, *write)* but today Nani insisted he accompany the family to the beach. "It's *ohana* time," she said, her expression stern. He knew he'd better not argue. He slipped into his sandals, reached for the straw hat Maria had given him, and helped Lucy into the back seat of the van with the dogs and the blonde. His work would be there when he returned.

Nani was waiting in the front passenger seat as Henry settled behind the wheel. He frowned at the filthy windshield, got out, sprayed the glass with window cleaner, and wiped down the suds with paper towels. For an old VW, the van had survived a great deal, and he was fond of it. It still ran, sort of. He turned the ignition, and for once it caught at the right moment. They headed for Hamoa Bay.

They drove through pasturelands ringing the volcano, the upper flank covered with dense forest, the peak silhouetted against the sky. "Earth touching heaven," Maria had said. She had written a poem about it. He wondered where it was.

"See, Princess," Lucy cried from the back seat, waking him from his thoughts, "the cows." They dotted the slopes, black spots against the green.

Soon the sea spread before them, they turned left, and descended to the cove.

The surf washed onto a crescent of gray sand bounded by volcanic rock, a beach James Michener decreed "perfect." To Henry, though, its beauty belied the powerful tides that swept smug locals and naive tourists out to sea. It was another example of nature's treachery—

beautiful and false outsides disguising ugly and true insides—and he was continually amazed at man's inability to see beyond the surface of things, or, in this case, beneath the shimmering waves to the deadly undertows. They lived under a volcano, in a paradise surrounded by drowning waters.

It was a perfect March day; the skies had cleared to a startling blue. The mountain still held slips of cirrus close, and in the opposite direction, where the horizon met the sea, a few wispy strands lingered. Henry parked the van on the shoulder of the road. They unloaded hampers and towels and gear, descended steep steps to the shore, and chose a quiet spot at the far end of the beach. There, under a shade tree, Nani spread out quilts and towels and Henry unfolded low canvas chairs as the dogs watched, waiting.

Only a few sunbathers had propped umbrellas on the sand, but soon, Henry knew, local teenagers would arrive, parking their trucks and scooters on the road above. A shuttle from the hotel would unload tourists, and the peace would be broken by rock music from radios and screams of children in the surf.

The blonde stripped to her bikini, what there was of it, and Henry looked out to sea, stroking Eli and scratching Alabar's ears. He felt her eyes on him but tried not to return her gaze. He turned away from the dogs and concentrated on plunging their umbrella pole into the sand and helping Lucy with her life vest, remembering to put her headband back on...all routine chores that calmed him. Meredith was a real piece of work, but an exquisite one, he had to admit, and even with her wounded face, her body was nearly perfect.

He turned to Nani. "When do you want lunch?" He spoke too abruptly, he thought with regret.

"You decide, Henry, you decide." Nani poured sunscreen onto her palms, rubbed them together, and ran her hands over Lucy's cheeks, arms, and legs. "Did you put on sunscreen, Henry?"

"Of course." He wished she would stop nagging about his skin, but knew she meant well. He'd had several growths removed over the years, but nothing malignant. He always lathered on sunscreen at home where he had a good mirror, careful not to miss a centimeter. He simply had a few freckles, and his tutu worried needlessly.

Nani looked relieved, as though she had checked one more item off her list. "I'm taking Lucy down to the water with the dogs. Where's her bucket and shovel?"

"Here somewhere." Henry looked around the cluttered array of baskets and totes.

"I've got them." Meredith held up a red plastic bucket with its yellow shovel. Her golden hair caught the light as she handed them to Nani.

"We'll be back soon," Nani said as she took Lucy's hand.

"We'll be back soon," Lucy repeated. She grinned at Henry and waved at Meredith.

Meredith stretched out on a quilt in the sun, one leg angled for balance. Henry moved his chair under the umbrella, adjusted his glasses, and pulled out his Eliot.

They remained silent for a time, the waves lapping the shore, and Henry found he was reading the same lines again and again:

> There is only the fight to recover what has been lost
> And found and lost again and again: and now, under conditions
> That seem unpropitious. But perhaps neither gain nor loss.
> For us, there is only the trying. The rest is not our business...

Only the trying. He lifted his eyes to the sea. His grandmother and daughter sat on the edge of the shore, tossing wood into the rippling waves for the dogs to retrieve. Henry watched Nani, suddenly thankful for his tutu. She wore loose beige shorts and a faded orange shirt. Her silver hair was braided down her back at an odd angle; Lucy must have helped, or Nani's arthritis was acting up. His tutu sat cross-legged, chattering constantly, watching Lucy throw a twig into the waves and dig with her shovel, her face determined. Lucy looked up from time to time to Nani, as though holding the old woman's words, and then returned to shoveling and tossing.

"You read a lot," Meredith said, not moving her head, her eyes hidden behind oversized dark glasses.

"It's what I do," he said. "I read in order to write, and in order to teach." Would he ever teach again? He was getting out of the academic loop. His sabbatical had become a leave of absence, an indefinite one.

"Why? Books aren't real."

She remained on her back, facing the open sky. Her skin, now lightly tanned, glistened with heat and lotion, and her breasts fell away from her chest, barely covered by the band of turquoise spandex. Her navel, pierced with a diamond, rose and fell with her gentle breathing. His eye continued down to the turquoise triangle over her pelvis and quickly back to her face. Her lips gleamed with gloss, and she had a freckle near her left ear. Her hair fanned like a golden halo. The bandages along her upper cheek and forehead gave her a vulnerable look.

"Of course they're real," he said.

"How can you say that? They're just words on a page."

Her moving lips mesmerized him. "Those words on a page answer the great questions. Don't you ever ask questions?"

"Ask questions? What questions?"

"The serious ones: the meaning of life, why we are here, why we suffer, how we choose to live our lives, what is truth, beauty, love, goodness, civility. For that matter, what is civilization itself, is our culture dying...what are the permanent values..." He'd given a pretty good lecture on that topic once. He wondered where the notes were. He could use them for Maria's book.

"Permanent values? Should *I* ask those questions?"

"We all should."

"That's rather pompous of you." She sat up and took off her glasses. Her blue eyes teased him as she leaned forward and wrapped her arms around her knees. He glimpsed her nipples.

"It's more like wishful thinking, a hope." He tried to pull his gaze away. He was suddenly sweating, praying for a breeze. He forced himself to look out to sea: the sky was still clear, but the clouds on the horizon were growing.

"Then tell me, oh wise professor who asks the right questions, why should these questions be asked? What difference does it make?"

He breathed deeply and smiled, latching onto the idea of their discourse, a mental ride he longed for. She was brighter than she let on.

"You did it." He turned toward her and focused on her wounds, her eyes, her hair. Her hair held many shades: amber, cream, streaks of copper.

"Did what?"

"You asked the right question."

"Come on, you haven't even answered me."

"Why must we ask? Because the answers determine how we form our society. Democracies depend on an *educated* electorate, people who understand the implications of their vote, understand what makes civilization *civil.*"

Meredith smiled with sudden recognition. Her teeth were white, her lips full, her face holding a surprising innocence. "That's what someone said at school. An *educated electorate.*" She sifted the sand through her fingers, lifting it and letting it pour through.

"Exactly. But no one asks the questions anymore. These issues are not part of popular debate, as they were, say, in the time of Eliot. Although he predicted our own age pretty accurately, I would say."

"And when was this, when everyone discussed life and death?"

He allowed his eyes to linger on her long neck, then, looking out to the horizon, he grasped his structures of thought for balance. "It's true it's been more of an upper-class, educated pursuit, and mostly prevalent at the turn of the nineteenth century." He sighed, wiping his brow. "But as early as the eighteenth...no, even the Renaissance...debate on these issues was widespread. It was part of the popular arts: the theater, for example."

"What about the Greeks and the Romans?"

"The classical world too. And many historians are finally recognizing the great debates of the Middle Ages, even crediting the twelfth-century Scholastics with the scientific method." He'd recently read Galileo's trial had been re-examined and the Catholic Church redeemed. Remarkable. He did miss his colleagues at the university.

"So why don't people talk about these things?"

He was enjoying himself, his face turned away, finally in control, knowing hers was fixed on him. "Three reasons, I think. One, our society has become all-inclusive and pluralistic. That is to say, in an effort to accept all beliefs, both religious and political, no one wants to argue about them. And two, in a democracy, the classes merge, so that the upper classes, those who once held the education degrees and saw themselves as the forum for debate, can no longer be defined. Three, and perhaps the most vital, is the disintegration of the family."

"Ah." She sounded overwhelmed.

"Do you follow me, Meredith?" He turned toward her. She was like one of his students. She lay on her back again, her hands on her tummy, her heels in the sand, her eyes closed against the sun.

"Sort of," she mumbled, her lips moist and glistening.

"Do you...agree?"

"I would add another reason," she said, rising on one elbow, "advertising."

He nodded. "We're drowning in words, dumbed-down words, simplistic phrases saying nothing, reducing great ideas, important ideas, to jargon. How can we possibly think, reflect?"

"I've heard most Americans read at the fifth-grade level."

"And publishers control what they read." He needed to contact *his* publisher, he thought. Their contract wasn't forever.

"What about TV? Short attention spans?"

"TV and movies become slapstick or vehicles of social agendas. Propaganda." He was getting depressed. Maybe she was right. Why bother? The obstacles were immense. He suddenly thought of Sammy and his debate club. Maybe that was what he was calling about. It might be fun to help him out. It was an election year, after all. Practice what he preached and educate the electorate. He'd call Sam when he got back.

"What about the universities?" She rolled onto her tummy. Her turquoise thong divided her buttocks. A bandage covered her thigh wound.

He wiped his brow. He could see Nani and Lucy walking along the beach and he willed them to return. "That's the last bastion of serious discussion: the university quarterlies, and similar publications, read by an elite group in ivory towers and assorted readers starved for ideas."

"But why do you blame divorce? Isn't that what you said?" she mumbled into the sand.

"I did...mention that." He glanced at the turquoise band running under her shoulder blades. Her skin was turning pink with the sun. He pulled out his pipe and studied it, cradling it in his palm, rubbing its bowl. He wouldn't smoke; he'd brought the pipe along simply to hold. He returned to his line of reasoning. "The entire family unit is under immense pressure, and divorce was the first deadly attack. When the traditional family separates, there is less of an oral tradition, less of any tradition, as new families form, split, and reform. The family was the perfect connection between past and present and future, through the generations." *I should be writing this down,* he thought. He was summarizing Maria's book.

"They were connected by oral tradition?" She glanced at him sideways.

"Like Nani-lei and her stories. She carries the answers to the questions in her stories, carries them into the next generation. It's a passing-on that cuts across class. And this passing-on is under attack."

"And here they come now." Meredith sounded relieved. "We'd better set out the picnic things."

They lunched on hot dogs, cole slaw, and fruit punch from the food shack. Nani slurped a banana shake and helped Lucy with her napkin and plastic fork. Henry dumped the garbage and returned to find Nani holding Lucy on her lap, rocking her gently. Meredith sat by her side, touching Lucy's hair.

Henry settled in his chair, closed his eyes, and dug his toes in the sand, ready for Nani's story. The sound of the waves washing the shore and Nani's melodic voice soothed him. The blonde was unnerving, their conversation upsetting.

"Tell the story of Maui and the mountain, Tutu Nani," Lucy said sleepily.

"Ah," Nani said, "the story of Maui and Haleakala. It's a very ancient story, about the demigod and his mother. You see, Maui's mother worked all day, but the day was not long enough to dry her tapa cloth and prepare her food. The sun moved through the sky too fast. So the young Maui thought of a plan."

"What did he do, Nani?" Lucy asked as she always asked.

"Maui noticed that the sun had sixteen long legs, and every morning it slipped one leg at a time above Haleakala until it reached the open sky. So Maui climbed the mountain."

"He climbed Haleakala?"

"He did. He climbed in the dark before sunrise and hid on top of the mountain, waiting for the first rays of the sun to appear."

"What did he do then, Nani?"

"He brought sixteen ropes, and as each ray came over the edge of the volcano, he lassoed it and tied it to a wiliwili tree."

Lucy clapped. "He tied up the sun!"

"Yes, my little Lucy, he tied up the sun, a very smart thing to do."

Henry heard Meredith laugh and say, "Clever Maui."

"Clever Maui," Lucy repeated. "What happened then?"

"You can imagine, the sun was angry, and he pleaded with Maui to untie him. 'You must promise me something, first, before I untie you,' clever Maui said to the sun. 'What is that?' asked the sun. 'You must promise to travel across the sky more slowly to give my mother more time.' And the sun agreed."

"Did Maui let the sun go?"

"He did, but he left some of the ropes tied to the sunrays to remind the sun of his promise. And every evening, as the sun sets, during the *ahiahi*, you can see the ropes of the sun trailing into the heavens."

"The *ahiahi*," whispered Meredith.

"Red ropes," Lucy said quietly. She blinked and rubbed her eyes with her knuckles.

"And that is why Haleakala is called the *House of the Sun*."

Nani stroked the child's hair and slipped off the headband. "Nap time, Lucy," she whispered as she kissed her on the forehead. Humming softly, she lay down beside her.

Henry watched them as a radio blared in the distance. He nodded to Meredith.

"Want to walk?" He called the dogs.

"Sure." She stood slowly and wrapped a pareo around her hips. "Wish I could swim—but not yet, I guess." She ran her finger along her cheek and glanced at her leg. "Still have to keep these dry. Maybe one day. San Francisco's ocean is too cold to swim most of the time."

They waded in the shallows. Eli darted in and out of the waves as Alabar ran along the shore. Henry glanced at her slim form matching his pace; her long legs glided through the clear water. He tossed a twig toward Eli.

"So, Henry," Meredith said, "was Nani's story one of your passing-on stories?"

Her tone was part tease, part challenge, part disbelief. Her flippancy was both exciting and frustrating.

"It was."

"But it's only a bedtime story."

"It's a story, yes, and it isn't literally true. It's myth, and myth tells a different kind of truth, perhaps a greater truth, a more universal truth."

"And this myth? What does the harnessing of the sun have to do with truth?" She looked up at him and smiled.

It *was* a beautiful smile.

"It tells of man and nature, the eternal war between the two, the vital need for man to control his environment in order to survive. We often forget that, with today's indoor plumbing, electricity, and telephones."

"I see."

"The old Hawaiians were animists—that is, they deified the natural world. There was a god of the sea, a god of the forest, and so on. Many primitive peoples did this. It was a way to relate to the enormous powers in their lives."

"But they really believed the literal telling."

"They did, and since then we have found more effective ways to harness nature than to pray to spirits. Even so, we aren't always successful. People drown every year off this coast."

Meredith shivered and looked away.

He frowned. "How thoughtless of me, with your accident."

"It's okay." She turned and gently stroked his arm, looking up at him with her wide blue eyes.

He ran his hand down her hair and she pulled him close, kissing him lightly. Her tongue sent tremors through him.

"That's thank you, Professor, for an excellent lesson."

"We'd better get back," he said as he caught his breath.

Thirteen

Henry slept little that night and woke early, having replayed the kiss again and again in his mind. He fed the dogs and returned to his study with taro rolls and strong coffee, the house quiet as the first light filtered through the shutters. He soon heard Nani bustling in the kitchen with Lucy, getting her ready for church. He listened for the blonde. Did he want to hear her voice? Or her bare feet on the stairs? Certainly not.

He had sorted Maria's notes into categories of meaning: self-sacrifice, love, and goodness; beauty and truth; permanent values and the moral imagination. The threads were there. He simply needed to weave them together. Was it possible? Was it necessary? Yes, it was both.

He rummaged for a yellow notepad in the bottom drawer and came across a photo framed in koa wood. Hana-lani stood on the rise above the sea, Haleakala hovering behind, the sun setting, and Maria sat in the lounge on the verandah, waving. She had given the picture to him for Christmas many years ago. "To remind you of home," she said. The Berkeley fog had enshrouded their bungalow and they sat before a crackling fire in the small front room. *"You* remind me of home," he replied as he pulled her toward him, holding her cropped head in his hands and removing her glasses. She unbuttoned his shirt and nuzzled his chest.

But they had fought about the children she didn't yet want and he did. She needed her freedom to finish her doctorate. *"Later,"* she had insisted. "We have plenty of time, and you won't love me when I'm fat."

"I don't care about fat," he replied.

But they didn't have plenty of time, and somehow later eluded them, always ahead, beckoning. Maria turned thirty-five, thirty-six, thirty-seven. She finished her doctorate; she was promoted to full professor. She worked on a book.

And each year she lost weight.

"You skipped breakfast," he said one morning as she returned from jogging.

"I'm strong enough."

"You should eat something."

"Can't eat this early."

"Having lunch?"

"Sure."

He knew she was lying.

When her periods stopped, Henry panicked, and he insisted she see a doctor. "She needs more calories, Henry, that's all," the internist said. "It's really that simple. I told her that."

"She thinks she's fat."

"Then she needs counseling."

"Can you arrange it?"

"I'll try."

Maria had reluctantly agreed. She did want a child one day, and she knew something would have to change. She cut back on her frenetic schedule and ate more. They flew home to Hana-lani the summer of '95.

"We'll fatten the girl up, Henry," Nani had said, forcing a laugh to make him feel better. He could see she worried too.

"Please, Nani, do something. I can't stand by and watch her like this."

"I'll talk to the man upstairs."

"What?"

"God, Henry, God."

"Oh, right."

The following year Lucy Maria was born.

Henry set the photo on his desk and turned to the yellow pad. Nani and Lucy bustled in the front hall, little feet and big ones shuffling on the planked floor. He heard Nani's quiet voice gently urging. The front door clicked open, then closed. Once again the house was silent.

⌘ ⌘ ⌘

The blonde knocked and walked in, carrying coffee and a bottle of rum.

"Your door was open." She grinned.

He frowned, annoyed at the interruption. "A little early for rum, don't you think?"

"It's cocktail hour somewhere. Anyway, it's almost noon." She wore a thin red tee that clung to her nipples. Her Capri pants straddled her hips. "Have your coffee straight then." She leaned over and set the tray down.

He kept his eyes fixed on the yellow pad. "Thanks."

"The house is sure quiet. Where *is* everyone?"

"Church."

"Oh, right, it's Sunday."

She sat in the leather chair and crossed her legs, swinging her bare foot back and forth, tapping her fingernails on her mug. "Want to do something? Go somewhere?"

"Look, Ms. Campbell, I've got work here."

"Call me Meredith. Come on, Henry, you've got to get out. Take me...somewhere, Henry. Please?" She set down her mug, moved behind him, and gently massaged his shoulders with her thumbs. *"Take me* somewhere...or maybe," she whispered in his ear, her breath warm, "you'd like to go upstairs...since we've got the house to ourselves."

He groaned and shook her off abruptly.

"Okay, I get the hint," she said, throwing her arms in the air. "You can have your old research and books and papers...of dead people." She waved to the photograph.

He gasped. "This was, is, Maria's work! Don't speak of her like that!"

"Well, I'm *so sorry*. She *is* dead, after all. At least *some* of us are *living*."

"Get out! Just get out!" His heart raced.

"Sure, I'll get out. I just might book my flight right now. Been meaning to. I can see where I'm not wanted. Three weeks is three weeks too many in this backwater, crash or no crash."

She slammed the door behind her. His heart tight, he stared at the space where she had been. He returned to his Eliot and read slowly, one word at a time:

Encouraged by superficial notions of evolution,
Which becomes, in the popular mind, a means of disowning the past...

What had he done?

He found Meredith on the back verandah. "I apologize. I overreacted."

She looked up from the lounge but continued swinging, pushing her bare foot against the warped flooring. "It's okay, no problem. Anyway, I got through on the phone. I booked flights for a week from Wednesday. Hana—Kahului—San Francisco. That's the earliest I could get, but I'm wait-listed for anything sooner." Her voice sounded shaky but determined.

"Next week?" he said, his throat tight. "What about your cuts? Are they healed well enough?" He sat next to her, steadying the swing.

"Well enough, and I've got to get back to the city. The bills are piling up. Some of us have to work for a living."

"Do you have a job at present? Are you still with the investment firm?"

"No, I've got to look for one."

"Of course. Maybe I could help. I've got contacts in the Bay Area. Think you'd like to work at the university?"

"Maybe."

They sat in silence looking over the grass to the sea.

He touched her leg. "Meredith, I've been thinking. You were right."

"Oh?" Her blue eyes held traces of mock amazement.

"I've been carrying Maria into the world of the living far too long. It's this book, I suppose." He looked at his hands, clasped in his lap as though they held the answers.

"Finish the book," she said matter-of-factly. She waved one arm in the air, as though it were that simple.

"I can't seem to make much progress." He touched her shoulder.

"Meredith," he said softly. She turned. Her blue eyes still hinted defiance. He'd offer a truce. "I'll take you somewhere to make up for my rudeness. It's only right. We can see another of our local wonders." He smiled his best smile and tilted his head, hoping he looked inviting.

She raised her brows, as though nothing could compensate for his behavior. "How about the Seven Sacred Pools? I've heard they're spectacular."

Startled, Henry hesitated. The site was a favorite of Maria's. "You mean Oheo Gulch up in Kipahulu Valley. There are more than seven, and they're no longer considered sacred, but they are indeed beautiful. Yes," he said, determined not to let this chance slip away as well, "we'll do it." He rose to his feet and offered his hand.

"And bring Nani and Lucy...and the dogs to chaperone us." She squeezed his hand as she stood and winked.

He smiled cautiously. That was generous, or calculating, of her. "It's not that you aren't attractive. I'm simply not ready for this yet." He twisted his ring.

She placed her hands on her hips. "I understand, Professor, I truly do. Now, let me change into something more appropriate." Flashing him a grin, she swayed into the house.

He watched her retreating figure. Maria wouldn't want him to mourn forever. Lucy needed a mother. A week from Wednesday wasn't much time, but he would find a way to keep Meredith in Hana, at least a little bit longer.

Fourteen

The pools spilled down from Haleakala, one into another, through a deep gorge overflowing from winter rains. Henry found a flat rock where they could sit and watch the falls tumble into the sea. Lucy screamed in delight, holding Nani's hand, and the dogs scampered in and out of the low vegetation lining the ponds. Below, the sapphire ocean crashed and palms fanned against the sky; the sun filtered through the mist as rain clouds hovered over the mountain. Henry gazed beyond the black rock to the sea. *The air is so fresh here you can drink it,*" Maria had said.

"It's wonderful," Meredith said.

"And treacherous. A woman fell from that cliff last year." He pointed up the mountain.

Meredith untied her pareo and laid it on the rock. Henry found himself staring again at her bikini. This one was yellow.

Maria had been fifteen, he seventeen, the first time they came here alone, and she had brought a picnic lunch. She wore a yellow sundress with green piping, white cotton splashed with blossoms, and her long dark hair was pulled into a ponytail. He had driven his first car, a '62 Ford, and had trouble with the idle. It was the summer before he left for college.

Nani buckled Lucy's life jacket and took her hand. "Henry, we're going to look for sunrise shells. Eli, Alabar, come!"

"To make a pretty necklace," Lucy added.

"Good," Henry said. "We'll set out the lunch things. Lucy, wait, you forgot your headband." Lucy frowned as he fitted it on her.

"I don't need it for sunrise shells," Lucy complained, following Nani.

Henry watched them climb down the rocks to the water.

"Sunrise shells?" Meredith rubbed lotion onto her legs, navigating around the bandage.

"Langford Pectins. Gray, lavender, pink, yellow, orange. They're the prettiest and rarest shells in Hawaii. Nani is always looking for them. They're scallops and worth a bit to the collector."

Meredith handed him the lotion. "So, Henry, would it be too forward to ask you to do my back?"

Her eyes were large and innocent, the long lashes dark and curled, the lids dusted in a pale blue that set off her irises. "Sure," he said as she turned around. "I mean, not at all. Not too forward, that is." Was he stuttering?

He poured a bit of the cocoa butter on his hands and massaged the lotion into her soft skin. Her shoulders moved gently in response and she sighed softly. He moved down her spine, letting his fingers slip under her arms, then under her strap and down to the small of her back.

"You have beautiful skin," he said, handing her the bottle.

"Thanks. You have nice hands." She turned and touched his lips with her finger. "You forgot your hat."

"Yes, I forgot my hat." His mind had turned to mush.

He kissed the back of her hand and brushed her lips lightly. She wrapped her arms around his neck, pulling him closer, and gently he tasted her mouth. His hands held her bare waist and drifted down toward her bikini.

He came up for air as his glasses fogged. "Meredith, you're so lovely...I don't want to hurt your face...."

"Not to worry, Professor." She grinned and pulled away. "Anyway, we've got to put out the lunch things, remember?"

"Right."

"How's the book coming? Get a lot done this morning?" She turned to the picnic hamper.

"Not really." Henry breathed deeply, watching her, wondering, seeing Maria again, as though in a trance.

"It's about asking the right questions?" She was handing him things, picnic things.

He began to set out plates and utensils and plastic containers, lining them up on the flat rock. "It's the history of ethics, of the desire or imperative to be good. You know, to do the right thing."

"I say, if it feels good, do it. It must be right."

He raised his brows. "That's just the problem."

"Oh?" She was fussing over the napkins, weighting them down with pebbles.

"Sometimes feeling good about a behavior doesn't mean it's morally right. The parameters are larger than that, even if we don't always see them."

"So what is goodness, what is right and wrong?"

"The Jews say the Ten Commandments."

"The Christians, too, I thought."

"The Christians add a few more: humility, sacrifice, other virtues, and their opposites which they call sins. These, too, came from Jewish precepts laid down long before Christ." He sat on a boulder and watched her arrange things on a gingham tablecloth.

"Like the Seven Deadly Sins?" She opened small plastic containers of food and slipped serving spoons into them.

"Can you name them?"

"I don't think so." She handed him a bottle of pickles to open.

"Pride, envy, anger, lust, sloth, gluttony, covetousness."

"I'm impressed."

"Want to know the Four Cardinal Virtues?" He gave her back the jar, the lid loose.

"Can't wait."

"Justice, prudence, temperance, fortitude."

"You're just brilliant, Professor. Now, slice this cheese." She handed him a small cutting board and paring knife.

He shoved the sharp blade through the thick mozzarella. "I sometimes think that if everyone avoided the first list and practiced the second, we'd have some kind of utopia, with no need for laws. There'd be no wars either, just peace."

Meredith wrinkled her brow in thought. "You may be right. No diets required if we avoid gluttony. And most crime is caused by anger."

"And pride, lust, envy, and covetousness. Forms of greed really." He recalled his father saying all sin was a kind of idolatry; maybe that was what he meant. "But humility is probably the most powerful one."

"Humility? No one believes in that anymore."

"Not today. Self-esteem has replaced humility."

"And sacrifice?"

"Sacrifice is largely gone as well. One can't look out for one's self and still sacrifice one's self for others. But many hold both opposing ideals and don't think twice."

"I suppose that's true." She opened two beers and handed him one as her brow wrinkled in thought. "And you, Henry, are you humble?" She ran her finger along his leg.

He sipped his beer. "I doubt it. Nor am I capable of sacrifice. I wish I were. I'd like to be made out of that kind of stuff." He looked away, recalling his father once again.

"Who is? You'd have to be a bloody saint."

He smiled ruefully. "My parents were saints, and bloody too." That was a little blunt, he thought. A little irreverent.

"Really?" She squinted at him with disbelief.

In his mind, Henry saw the letter he carried up the front steps of Hana-lani, postmarked Singapore, the smudged address, the curious foreign stamps. He had opened it slowly, certain the thin pages held an unknown terror.

He worked to control his voice. "My parents were missionaries in Indonesia. They were killed by terrorists." *Everyone I love dies.* Self-pity stabbed him.

"I'm sorry." Her voice held genuine sorrow. "How old were you?" She sat down next to him.

"Twelve."

He had read the words on the crinkly onionskin and screamed for Tutu Nani. Maria stood next to her grandmother, clutching her hand, her dark eyes on Henry. She dropped Nani's hand and hugged him, her thin arms wrapping around his waist. He'd pushed her away and fled into the taro fields, out to the cliff, and down to the tide pools. Nani had found him there, and they sat together on the rocks, weeping and looking out to sea.

He shook his head. Even today, forty years later, the loss was overwhelming.

"They were missionaries? But you aren't religious, are you?"

"Should I be? Their faith killed them." Blunt again.

"At least they weren't hypocrites. They practiced what they preached. Or they tried to."

Henry frowned. "And you would say if you don't live up to your ideals you're a hypocrite?"

"Well—"

"A person with any standards at all necessarily becomes a hypocrite. No one can entirely practice what they preach. That's the problem today. There are so few hypocrites. We've lowered the bar so that we can be 'true' to ourselves, whatever that means." He stared out to the horizon, aware his voice was rising. She had hit a nerve. His colleagues at the university had belittled the Victorians, saying they were hypocrites. Henry saw it differently. They simply had noble ideals and were human, a far better social construct than no ideals at all, like in the animal world. Today's construct was bestial at best.

"Sorry." Meredith examined her nails. "No need to get all worked up."

I'm sorry." He turned and kissed her lightly on the forehead. "The important thing is to try, I suppose." *Only the trying.* Is that what Eliot had meant? "Speaking of saints and trying, did you know we have a Hawaiian on Rome's potential saint list? Father Damien."

"Damien? Was he the one who lived on the leper island?"

"Right. Molokai. One could say he *tried* to practice love, to practice sacrifice." Henry looked at his mottled hands and arms. "I can't imagine what that must have been like."

"I saw a movie about him."

"In the end he died of the disease. He wasn't that old either." Henry recalled the biography he had read as a boy. Nani had given it to him after one of his biopsies had come back. He rubbed his cheek where the scar was, where they had cut the tissue away.

Meredith looked toward the horizon. "My brother had ideals like that."

Henry swallowed hard. He hoped he hadn't opened an old wound. Wounds were best left covered, at least until they scabbed. "How so?" he asked gently.

"He died in the Persian Gulf."

Henry groaned. "I'm sorry again." He shook his head.

"Dylan and I weren't close. Nevertheless, he *was* my brother. He was older, by four years. He went to live with my dad pretty early on. We were...different."

Henry realized how little he knew about Meredith. "You were right, though. He sacrificed himself for his, for our, country. Our military are a perfect example of love, patriotic love."

"Thanks," she said. Her eyes held gratitude. "That's nice, really nice."

"To my mind, we can't honor them enough."

She nodded, her eyes glazed with memory.

He tried to bring her back. "At any rate, my parents were simply in the wrong place at the wrong time."

She turned and touched his arm. "I admire their commitment, Henry. I admired Dylan's. I've never felt that sort of thing. Your folks must have been so sure, their lives so full of meaning. You know, no doubts about stuff."

Henry threw a pebble into the pool and watched it sink into the spinning froth. He hadn't thought of his parents in that light before. They had been irrational beings to him, leaving him when he needed them, dying like that. It was so unnecessary, he thought. *Such a waste.*

"And you, Meredith, do you believe in anything, any kind of ideal?"

"I believe in love."

He laughed. "That's good. That's *really* good."

"I *do* believe in love. What's wrong with that?"

"And what is love?"

"I could show you." She ran her finger down his back. Her nail tickled through his shirt.

"That, my dear, is *lust.*"

"Same thing, silly."

"*Not* the same thing. Love is an overused word. It *should* mean all that our world denies. It should mean sacrifice for the beloved, nothing less."

"How noble. Do you really believe that?"

"I do. Otherwise it's merely *like* or *lust* and not *love.*"

"So do you...lust...love...you know, *do it...*, Henry?"

She was certainly direct.

"Do what, exactly?"

"You know, get a little?"

"Get a little? Now what would you mean by that?" He was enjoying this. She was deadly serious.

"Sex, Henry, sex." She raised her brows and sighed, as though he were an idiot.

"Oh, *that's* what you mean. No, but I've made love, which is a different thing to my mind." How sad he suddenly felt, how grieved over their dying language, the coarsening of words and phrases, a reflection of something larger, a cancer devouring civilized culture. The words tore at his sensibilities, at times outraging him. When did making love become having sex? The most sublime act between man and woman was equated to eating a hamburger, probably takeout, on the run. A physical need that must be met. They were becoming animals, nothing more.

Meredith looked at him as though he were a creature from another world. "Right. Glad to hear you're getting a little." She smiled as she adjusted her swimsuit top.

Something rustled in the bushes.

"They're back," she said, reaching for her pareo.

Lucy pulled Nani by the hand. The dogs trailed close behind, sniffing the ground.

"Look, Papa!" Lucy jumped up and down. She emptied her plastic bag of shells, stones, and flowers into his lap.

Henry studied the assortment. "My, oh my, that's quite a collection."

"Very pretty, Lucy," Meredith said.

Lucy turned to Meredith. "I'm making a necklace for *you*, the pretty princess. It's going to be so cool."

"Thank you, I would like that."

Henry watched them. A picture of the future formed like pieces in a puzzle: old Nani, his daughter Lucy, and...Meredith. But did he *love* Meredith? Would he sacrifice for her? Or, more to the point, would she have a fellow old enough to be her father? Could *she* love *him?*

Fifteen

They lunched on leftover chicken, yogurt, sweet potato salad, and pineapple slices as the sun moved closer to the mountain. Henry and Meredith packed up, and Nani beckoned to Lucy. They found a patch of wild grass in the shade of a tall plumeria tree.

"Story time, Lucy," she said. She spread her quilt, and Lucy snuggled into her side.

Henry sat down, leaning back against the tree's smooth trunk, and Meredith stretched out, her head in his lap. He touched her hair, moving the long plaits to frame her face, and she smiled up at him as though life could be as simple as this moment, enjoy it. Was it that simple? Could he enjoy it? He glanced at the dogs. They too were content. Eli snored and Alabar chewed his paws for fleas.

"Tell the story of the princess," Lucy said as she watched Meredith and her father.

"Ah," Nani said, "you mean Princess Kapiolani."

"Princess Kapiolani." Lucy clapped her hands and adjusted her headband.

Henry reminded himself to ask his daughter about the headband. She seemed uncomfortable with it. It probably needed adjusting.

Nani breathed deeply and wrapped her arm around Lucy.

"Long ago," she began, "the great King Kamehameha conquered the many islands of Hawaii and made them one kingdom. This was good, for the peoples no longer made war with each other. When Kamehameha died, his brother, Liholiho, became king alongside Queen Kaahumanu. They did great things too."

"What did they do?"

"They did away with the old religion."

"Were the people angry?"

"Some were angry. But the women were happy. Under the old

religion, the women were not allowed to eat with the men. If they did, they would die. And...they were not allowed to eat certain foods."

"What foods?"

"Foods like bananas."

"I love bananas," Lucy said as she rubbed her eyes.

"The women of old did too. So Liholiho destroyed the *heiau*, the pagan temples, and he tore down the wooden statues of the old gods. But one god, or rather, goddess, still held power over the minds of the people."

"Who was that, Tutu Nani?" Lucy asked.

"Her name was Pele, and she was a fire goddess. She lived in the volcano called Kilauea, which sends fire into the sky to this day. But the Princess Kapiolani believed in the missionaries' God, the Christian God, the Lord God Jehovah. So the princess challenged Pele. She climbed through forests and old lava flows to the top of Kilauea, carrying a book the missionaries gave her. Many others followed to see what would happen. At the top of the volcano, they looked down into the boiling lava, where steam hissed and fire burned."

Lucy's eyes grew big. "What happened then?"

"The princess began to sing, and the people sang with her. They sang hymns to the Lord God Jehovah. And then the princess did a dangerous thing. She ate some sacred Ohelo berries that grew on the side of the mountain."

"Was Pele angry?"

"Patience, little one, and you will see. The princess cried out to the people, 'Jehovah is my God! He kindled these fires. I fear not Pele. If I perish by the anger of Pele, you may fear the power of Pele. But if I trust in Jehovah, and he shall keep me from the wrath of Pele, you must believe in the Lord Jehovah. The gods of Hawaii have no power.' If Pele was real, she would erupt with fire. But nothing happened. From that time on, the people no longer feared Pele, the fire goddess of the volcano. They were free."

"They were free!" Lucy clapped her hands.

"And humans," Henry whispered to Meredith, "were no long sacrificed on her altar."

Lucy now lay in the crook of Nani's arm, and Nani slipped off her headband. Humming, she settled her granddaughter on the quilt.

Henry led Meredith down to the cove below the pond. The dogs padded behind them.

"Did they really practice human sacrifice?" Meredith asked.

"Many primitive peoples practiced human sacrifice. The idea of a perfect, innocent, blood sacrifice, all three qualities necessary, to atone for man's sins is widespread. The ancient Hebrews sacrificed young, unblemished animals to atone for their collective guilt."

"But they don't anymore," Meredith said. She took his hand to step down onto the pebbly beach.

"No, but there is evidence that satanic rituals include such bloodshed, and living sacrifice can still be found in the rites of primitive tribes of Asia and Africa. Christians, of course, claim their Christ was an all-sufficient perfect, innocent, blood sacrifice." He was oversimplifying, he knew, but this was not the time and place for the finer points of atonement theology.

They walked along the shore. The afternoon shadows dappled the sands, the moist air heavy with promised rain. He slipped his arm around her, conscious of his flabby tummy, his thick glasses.

"This is so beautiful." Meredith stared out to sea, her arm around his waist. "How do you manage any time at all in your office?" She tossed a stick into the water and the dogs swam out to retrieve it.

"It is beautiful, isn't it?" He breathed deeply, focusing, beyond the dogs, on an outrigger moving toward the horizon. When had he last noticed a canoe?

"The sun," she said, "is heading for the mountain. You have an early sunset here."

"And an early sunrise over the sea."

"The aromas are incredible. What is it I smell *now*?"

He inhaled the breeze, considering. "Gardenia, I believe."

"It's lovely." She turned to him and pulled him toward her.

"Meredith," he whispered. Their lips brushed, tantalizing.

"Don't talk, Henry, just love me." She lay her pareo on the sand in the shelter of a hibiscus bush. She took off her bikini.

He stared.

"Don't you like me?"

"You're very attractive, but...here?"

She took his hand and pulled him down onto the cloth. "Here, Henry, now."

Henry slipped off his shorts and shirt, and set his glasses carefully on top of the neatly folded pile. Hungry, he gazed at her body. She lay on her side, waiting, running her fingers along the tops of her breasts, then lightly over her pelvic hair, blond and curly. Her skin glistened, and a red flush was forming on her chest and moving up her neck. Her hair, damp from the humidity and heat, fell away from her face like corn silk. She waited, watching him. Did she notice his white flab? He lay beside her and wrapped her with his body, feeling her warm skin against his. She rested her good cheek against his chest, sighed deeply, and turned her face to kiss him, a long, paralyzing kiss.

"Meredith, Meredith," he whispered in her ear. "I've been so lonely."

"I know, Henry, I know."

He allowed himself to ride the wave. Where was he going? Did he care?

⌘ ⌘ ⌘

That night Henry tiptoed to Meredith's room, carefully opened the door, dropped his robe, and slipped into the bed. She turned toward him.

"You're here at last."

"Will you sleep with a bookish old man?"

"Will you sleep with a brazen young woman?"

"Brazen but beautiful."

He pulled her close, running his hand down her narrow waist.

"I'll take care with your cuts," he said. "Extra care. I don't want to hurt you, darling. Tell me if I do."

"I'm fine, Henry. Just love me."

Sixteen

Monday morning Meredith woke and ran her hand over the indentation on the pillow. She smiled. She had won, and for the moment, the void, the emptiness, was filled. He would help pass the time. He would keep her sane, keep her away from the edge, at least until her flight home.

Every man had a weakness, and she had found Henry's—his books and his learning. During the day, she would play student, a new experience for her, at least outside the classroom. And how she adored new experiences. In the night he would steal up the creaking stairs, and for a few hours she would teach and he would learn, a neat twist on variety, secretly holding class in the old featherbed.

She descended the stairs to breakfast. Nani and Lucy sat with Henry at the dining table. She checked Henry's finger. He still wore his wedding ring. Good.

"Aloha, Ms. Campbell," Henry said. His eyes were bright with understood innuendos. "It's a beautiful day."

"Good morning, all." She took the seat next to him, unfolded her napkin over her bare legs, and ran her hand over Henry's knee under the table. "Sleep well?"

Henry blushed and looked at his papaya.

Nani bowed her head, clasping her palms. Lucy clapped hers together, and her grandmother said grace. Henry passed the toast and Meredith poured the guava juice.

Henry recovered his composure. "Let's hike up to Waimoku Falls. What do you say, Meredith?"

Nani looked up, and Meredith sensed she guessed their new relationship.

"I'll take Lucy to my quilting group," Nani said. "She'll be with other children, and she needs that. I'll bring the dogs too. The children love them, and Bess has a big back yard."

"Do you need a ride?" Henry asked.

"Sammy's picking me up in the truck, bless the boy. Miss Meredith, will you read to Lucy this morning, before you go?"

"I'd love to," Meredith said. She winked at Henry.

"Maybe," Henry said to Lucy, "we can convince the princess to postpone her flight home."

"Yes! Yes!"

"It would be good for us, Miss Campbell," Nani said, "if you stay a bit longer?"

Meredith grinned. This was easier than taking candy from a baby. "I'd like that," she said, eyeing Henry. She even had him volunteering to leave his books. He was becoming a real tour director. And his grandma approved.

"Then it's settled." Henry laid his palm firmly on the table.

She would confirm her flight and touch base with Parker first chance. Things were looking up.

⌘ ⌘ ⌘

After breakfast Meredith stepped into the library, looking for Lucy. She found the child perched precariously on the top rung of a stepladder, reaching for a book.

"Lucy!" she gasped. Meredith raised her arms to help her down. "Come down slowly. I'll help you."

"But the story—"

"Point to which one and I'll get it."

Lucy pointed to a large volume, turned, and dropped into Meredith's body. The child was warm, and her thin arms wrapped around Meredith's shoulders as she buried her head in her chest. Meredith felt the rapid beat of Lucy's heart.

"Thank you," Lucy said as her feet touched the floor.

Meredith opened the book. Glossy pages were covered with vivid illustrations in purples, blues, reds, and greens: *The Children's Book of Virtues*. They settled side-by-side into a wing chair.

"Read, please." Lucy adjusted her yellow headband and tapped her finger on the shiny page. "I'm ready."

Meredith scanned the Table of Contents. "Which one? Mmm...let's see...'The Tortoise and the Hare'...'The Little Red Hen'...'The Lion and the Mouse'...'The Boy Who Cried Wolf'..."

"'The Little Red Hen.'"

As Meredith read the story of the industrious hen who planted, reaped, threshed, ground, and baked without the help of her friends, a curious calm settled upon her. Lucy's warm body nestled into hers, and the child's eyes moved from the page to Meredith's face and back to the page. For the moment they were one, she and the child, connected by a voice and a page.

Meredith paused at the end. "Do you know the moral of the story?"

"If you want to eat the bread," Lucy said, as she wound a curl around her finger, "you have to help make it." She swung her legs back and forth.

Meredith smiled. She put her arm around the child's shoulders, feeling the tiny bones. "Good. Now which one?"

"The Boy Who Cried Wolf," she said. "Please."

As Meredith turned to the page, Lucy reached for her wounded cheek and lightly traced the edges of the bandages. "I had a boo-boo once."

"Did you? I'm sorry."

Lucy rubbed her hands sagely and nodded.

"Where was your boo-boo?" Meredith asked.

"Here," she said, tapping her knee.

A tiny scar marked the smooth skin.

"What happened?"

"I fell down. At the tide pools. The rocks cut me. See?"

Meredith patted her knee. "But it's all better now?"

"Nani kissed it and made it well. Do you want me to kiss your boo-boo, Princess?"

Meredith smiled. "Sure."

Lucy placed her hands on each side of Meredith's head and gently pulled her face toward hers. She kissed the bandages lightly. "Now you will be better for sure."

Meredith swallowed hard. "Thanks."

She turned to the story.

⌘ ⌘ ⌘

Sammy arrived at ten and let himself in. "I'm early. Reading to Lucy?"

Meredith looked up from the picture book as he paused in the entryway. "I'll have her ready in a minute. We just finished." She set down the book and took Lucy's hand.

"Actually, I wanted to see Henry first."

"Oh?"

"Is he in his study?"

"I think so."

Sammy looked at her wounds. "How are you feeling? Want me to check these?"

"They're fine." Meredith thought he looked nervous.

"How's Henry doing?"

"Pretty good." *Actually, he's great,* she thought, smiling inside.

"I heard you went to Oheo Gulch? Nice there." He looked at the floor.

Lucy was pulling on Meredith's hand.

"Henry's been kind enough to show me around a bit."

"Planning to stay on for a while?" He seemed worried as he glanced down the hall toward Henry's study.

"I have a flight out next week."

"Oh...I'm sorry. Lucy likes you." He fiddled with a wide ring on his right hand. Meredith thought it might be a class ring.

She grinned and looked down at the child. "And I like Lucy. But I've got to find a job back home."

He sighed and looked into her eyes. "I know what that's like." He raised his brows. "What do you do, Meredith?"

She thought for a moment. "I'm not sure, to tell you the truth. I worked in investment banking for a while. I helped with my mother's fashion business. That was fun."

"I think you'd be good with people."

Meredith smiled. If he only knew *how* good she was with people. But maybe she really wasn't that good. She thought of Nick. She thought of Mapleton firing her. She shook her head. "I'm not so sure."

"You're beautiful and you're bright. You could do anything you want."

"Thank you, but do you really think so?"

"Absolutely."

Meredith paused, then said, "I think I'd like to produce something, really set something up, make it run, like with people doing real things."

Sammy raised an appreciative brow. "Sounds like you might be a good manager. All you need to do is figure out what you want to manage."

"Yeah." She was right back where she started, which was nowhere. But she did need to think about employment. Maybe she should go back to school. College had been a lot of fun. Maybe Aunt Julia would help out again. "Sammy, what does Henry do for money? How does he live? Am I being nosy?"

Nani appeared in the doorway and nodded to Sammy. "We'll be ready soon. Lucy, come here, my little one."

Meredith released Lucy's hand, and the child ran to her grandmother. Sammy sat down in one of the wicker chairs. Meredith took the other.

He leaned toward her, resting his broad palms on his knees. He wore denims and work boots and a white polo shirt. His eyes were soft brown, slightly slanted, and he looked at her as though giving a report, an accounting, a summation of Henry's means. "It's okay. Henry's situation is no secret. Hana-lani is Lucy's, in trust. The property got grandfathered through several wills. My dad handled the last one in Kahului."

Meredith nodded. "You don't have to tell me all this."

Sammy shook his head. "You've grown close to the family. I can tell. You may as well know the whole picture. And I know Henry can be perplexing sometimes, like he's off on cloud nine."

Meredith grinned. "You can say that again."

"So Henry lives here in Lucy's house. He doesn't have much else, really. He has royalties from a textbook he wrote awhile back. I think he had life insurance on Maria. He and Nani have few needs, and they manage on what they have. Nani has a small pension, a fisherman's fund, and Social Security."

"I see," Meredith said. "It's always been a struggle for me, and I wondered about Henry. My life has been rather hand to mouth. My folks too." Except for her father's wild ride through Wall Street.

He nodded in agreement. "Me too. I do find working for something makes me value it more. But..." His eyes twinkled with a secret. "I've got great news. I made an offer on a house halfway between here and Kahului. *My first house.*" He rubbed his hands as though he couldn't believe it. "I wanted to buy one before I turned thirty but didn't make it. Still, I'm only five years late."

"Congratulations. This would be closer to Hana?"

"Exactly. I want to spend two days here, not one, and cut back on the Kahului time, maybe increase the staff and funding here. The Hana clinic fills up way too fast."

Meredith recalled she had been transferred from the clinic. "I guess it does. But I'm glad I came here." She looked down the hall to Lucy's room. "And I'm glad Hana-lani is Lucy's. It seems appropriate. When will she come into her inheritance?"

"When she's twenty-one. But Nani wants her to share it with Hana School."

"Hana School?"

"You know, let them use the house for exhibits or special events. That kind of thing. Maybe let them use the grounds for a botanical garden. There's quite a few acres here. She hasn't convinced Henry yet. Can't find the appropriate time, I suppose."

"He's been pretty withdrawn, hasn't he?" *Until now,* she thought, once again smiling inside.

He nodded. "In fact, the reason I wanted to see him wasn't just to see how he was doing. I actually had an ulterior motive."

"Oh?" It was difficult to see Sammy Tagami as scheming.

He pulled out a flyer from his back pocket. "Our Debate Club has grown. We can't meet at the grill anymore. That's good news, I guess."

"Where will you go?"

"I thought it might be nice to meet here. And it would open the door to Nani's plans."

Meredith wondered what a debate club actually debated. "What do you talk about?"

Sammy looked thoughtful. "The topics change all the time, and we try taking different sides. But with the primaries coming up, we could debate the issues. Henry should like that, and he needs to be around more people, get outside himself."

She laid her hand on his. "You're a good friend to Henry, Dr. Sam."

A light flush rose in his cheeks and he moved his hand away. "We've been friends since I was little. He's been more like an uncle to me. He was my family in Berkeley. I've been worried about him since he came back, since Maria...." He wrung his hands and looked away.

Nani appeared with Lucy. "Can we go, Sammy? I said I'd be early today."

Sammy rose. Disappointment shadowed his face. "Sure. I'll see Henry next time. Could you give him this flyer, Meredith? And mention my idea?"

Meredith took the flyer, nodding, and watched the three troop out the front door. She climbed the stairs, considering what she would wear. They were hiking up a mountain to waterfalls. This could be intriguing.

Seventeen

It was nearly noon when they stopped at Hasegawa's General Store. The front of the old movie theater was covered in faded posters, peeling at the corners. Meredith followed Henry to a side entrance where want ads for jobs, items for sale, and yoga classes were tacked on a cork board. They moved up and down the crowded aisles of the old market as Henry filled a basket with water, apples, and small rounds of Edam. Rakes and hoes, and other hardware Meredith didn't recognize, hung from the ceiling. Novels, local histories, and guidebooks crowded corner shelves, dry goods lined aisles, and in the back, vegetables, meat, and dairy products filled the cold cases. Dried fruit and candied ginger, sealed in cellophane, hung from rotating stands alongside chocolate bars, marshmallows, and trail mix. Baking supplies and kitchen equipment, greeting cards, Kona coffee, charcoal, matches, napkins—a jumbled assortment of goods—packed the barnlike space.

Henry toured the aisles as though he owned them, knowing each product's location. The cashier greeted him by name and several customers slapped him on the back in passing. It was like Brooklyn and Mr. Rosen's corner grocery, with Papa on Saturdays. Mr. Rosen knew her, called her "Little Miss Meredith," and she picked out an ice cream from the deep freeze and carried it carefully to the counter. Mr. Rosen included a free chocolate candy in the bag and waved as they left. "See you next time, Miss Meredith," he would say, the bell over the door jingling. She and Papa then walked to the park, she concentrating on her vanilla-on-a-stick covered in crispy chocolate, working her way from the bottom to the top as her father had taught her. "Bottom first; that way you catch the drips," he explained.

But there was no corner grocery near the tenth-floor apartment she and her mother moved to after the divorce, and even that apartment was soon abandoned for another across town when her mother changed boyfriends. They moved often, it seemed, and her classmates changed with each move. Restlessness became a way of life. She thought Parker was her longest friendship yet, going back to her college days. Even so, did she really know Parker? Did shopping and drinking constitute a friendship? *Probably as good as any,* she thought, and *maybe better than some.*

"Hasegawa's is a local institution," Henry said when they returned to the van. "It's been here as long as I can remember." He transferred the food to his backpack and folded the paper bag neatly.

"I'll bet Nani shopped here when she was little."

He smiled. "I don't think it's been here *that* long."

They drove down the coast and arrived at the Visitor Center, a single-story building in a modest parking lot. Henry strapped on his pack and locked the car. Meredith followed him to the trailhead, where a sturdy sign announced:

WILDERNESS TRAIL
EXPECT ROUGH, UNEVEN FOOTING
WHICH WHEN WET IS SLIPPERY.
STURDY FOOTWEAR RECOMMENDED.
CLIFF AREAS, STREAMS, AND POOLS
ARE HAZARDOUS. CLIFF JUMPING
HAS CAUSED INJURY AND DEATH.

"Injury and death?" Meredith asked.

"For those who don't use common sense."

"Are *these* shoes sturdy enough?" Meredith had little experience with hiking.

"Sure," Henry said, looking at her sneakers. "Did you put on sunscreen?"

"Sunscreen, of course," she said, lying. How could she tan if she put on sunscreen?

"Wear this." He handed her an old baseball cap.

She had tied back her hair with one of Henry's bandanas, a red paisley cotton, and now she slipped on his worn denim cap. At least it matched her cut-offs, which hung low on her hips, leaving her midriff bare under her white halter top.

"How far are the waterfalls?"

"Not too far." He shook his head as he gazed up the mountainside. "I haven't been up here in ages. This is great."

They headed up the dirt trail and into a dense forest. Tree roots twisted and broke through the earth. Massive trunks bordered the pathway. Branches spread in all directions, leafy tentacles welcoming, and blocking, the sun. The light that found its way through the foliage splashed the path, flickering, dancing with the shady patches.

Meredith stepped carefully over boulders and half-buried limbs, looking for footholds. Suddenly she tripped on a root and caught herself.

"You okay?" He waited for her to catch up.

"Sure," she said as she silently cursed the strange land. "They don't keep up the path very well, do they?"

"It's a National Forest. It's kept as natural as possible. These ancient trees are part of the native eco-system."

"Oh."

He turned back to the trail. "You go first, so I don't get ahead of you."

She passed him, and as she stepped carefully through the roots and rocks, she felt his gaze. She swayed her hips slowly, her legs rising and falling, and soon fell into a rhythm. She glanced back. He was perspiring. As he caught up with her, she turned and wrapped her arms around his neck. He kissed her softly.

Henry pulled himself away and breathed deeply. "We'd better keep going." He opened a bottle of water. "Here, have a sip."

The trail ascended through meadows and more forest, through still, steamy air. Their feet padded the earth. A bird cawed. Meredith half-expected to see Amazon warriors appear or monkeys swinging from trees. The air weighed heavily. Each step was like walking through a wall.

She paused and turned around. "How far is it now, Henry?" They'd been hiking for at least an hour.

"Can't be that much farther." He wiped his brow and pulled out the water bottle.

"It's after two." She shifted her watchband, which was sticking to her moist skin. Her makeup must have melted by now. She sneaked a look at the mirror in her pack. Her cheeks were flushed, rather attractive, really, and a bead of perspiration rested on her upper lip. Her hair had come loose from the bandanna and fell between her breasts. She looked like a young, blond Jane Seymour in the wild. She would be Jane, he Tarzan. She smiled, nearly tripping again as she started off.

They followed a planked walkway that bridged lowland.

"This meadow is swampy most of the year," Henry explained.

Suddenly a clattering filled the air, like bowling pins falling down, or blinds being drawn up.

"What's that sound?" Meredith asked.

"Wait—you'll see. It's coming from right around this bend."

At the end of the wooden path, walls of pale green reeds rose over fifty feet on either side of the trail.

"The bamboo forest." Henry paused.

"Amazing."

They walked between the tall clattering stalks.

"It grows like this?"

"Unusual, isn't it?"

"Wow."

"The falls are up ahead."

They emerged onto an open, grassy knoll looking over a deep canyon. A waterfall cascaded in frothy torrents down the rock face to pools below. The roar filled her ears.

"It's beautiful!" Meredith shouted.

He removed his cap and wiped his brow. "Stay away from the edge."

They stepped into a sheltered clearing. Sitting on a log, they unpacked the cheese and fruit and breadsticks. They ate silently as they watched the water and listened to the torrent.

His stare warmed her cheek. "Meredith, tell me about yourself."

"There's not much to tell."

"Do you have a family?"

"Yes and no. I once had a brother, as you know. My mother doesn't really want me around, and my father's in a rest home."

He fell silent. "I'm sorry."

"Don't be. I'm not. Anyway, Aunt Julia has looked after me over the years."

"Rather like my Tutu Nani."

"Not exactly. I haven't seen much of Julia either, but when my father ran through the small family trust, toward the end of wife number three, she helped me through college."

"Where'd you go?"

"Caulfield in New York. I grew up in Brooklyn. I was lucky to get in. Julia was an alumna and that helped."

"What was your major?"

"Basket weaving. Ha. Got you! No, it was close though. Art history."

"Really? So you do have some background in history."

"With an emphasis on the moderns."

"Oh. How did you end up with an investment banking firm?"

She laughed. If he only knew the story behind that one. "I pulled a few strings. My roommate from college helped. Her father is Kirby of Kirby and Calhoun."

"Really?"

"Know him?"

"Know of him."

"How so?"

"I'll tell you some day. Leave it to say, I admire him a great deal. He funded a professorship in my department at the university. There are some who think he should run for office."

"Some probably think *you* should run for office." She ran her hand down his cheek to the short beard. "I wonder what you look like without this."

"You might find out."

She pulled him close.

He slipped his finger through her hair and untied the bandanna. "You are so lovely."

He had removed his glasses, and his eyes were wide, searching. She brushed her lips against his.

He drew her to him and pulled her off the log, into the tall grass.

The falls thundered behind them as he kissed her neck, his lips moving slowly downward with a light touch, teasing.

⌘ ⌘ ⌘

It had been a new experience, making love near torrential falls, in the afternoon sun, in the grass, and Meredith held onto the moment as she padded down the path, Henry following close behind. She would add it to her memory album. She could not think of anything at home that compared. There was the time with Tod in the dunes off Monterey Bay, but it was chilly and the sand gritty. There was an encounter in the abandoned lighthouse at Point Reyes, probably Freddie, but that wasn't really *outdoors*, and the blanket had done little to soften or warm the cement floor.

This had been *jungle* love, she thought. Definitely unique. Once again she was grateful for the pill that took care of things, allowing her spontaneity. If she had believed in saints, the inventor of this little dial of colored tabs would definitely be her favorite. She chuckled.

"What do you find so amusing?" Henry paused beneath a twisted tree, its branches shooting horizontally like a giant fan. He kissed her lightly. "I want to know all your thoughts, darling, everything."

She looked at him. *You don't want to know all my thoughts, Professor.* And he was using the *darling* word, the ownership word. A fling was fine. Didn't he get it? She checked his finger. He still wore his ring.

"I don't know." She searched for an appropriate answer. "I was thinking about how amazing you were back there...you know...by the waterfalls."

He blushed. "And you were amazing too." He drew her near and ran his hand through her hair. "And how's your cheek? Does it still hurt?"

"A twinge every now and then, but it's almost healed, I'd say."

"That's good. You'll be back to your old self before you know it."

"We'd better get going." She touched the bandage and, for a brief moment, wondered who her old self was, after all. "'We don't want

Nani to worry."

"I'm looking forward to tonight."

"So am I." She stepped onto the trail. It was all an illusion, she thought, this contentment that crept upon her without warning. It was the islands, the mesmerizing skies and seas, the intoxicating aromas and paralyzing humidity. It was Henry too, but he was too old and too strange for her taste. Wasn't there a story about a fellow at sea who was hypnotized by the songs of women on shore? Oliver something? Odin? No, *Odysseus*, that was it. Henry and Hana-lani, Nani and Lucy, they were from another world. They were casting spells on her. They would swallow her whole.

⌘ ⌘ ⌘

They'd been walking far too long, Meredith thought. They must have made a wrong turn, for the path didn't look familiar, and Henry appeared worried. The sun was low, too low. She looked at her watch. It had stopped, the hands stuck at three-fifteen.

They came to an open field where the path ended and a dirt road began.

Henry paused and looked around. "I think we missed a turn. We can take this road through the pastures down to the highway. It's more direct."

"What time is it?"

"Nearly five."

"Any water left?"

"Sorry, we finished it off."

They followed the road, and Meredith cursed the dirt and the heat. Her skin was layered with a fine red dust and her muscles throbbed, beginning with her legs and working into her shoulders. She was sure her left heel must be raw from rubbing against the stiff canvas of her shoe. Was it bleeding? The cut on her thigh throbbed and her cheek wound burned. She wiped her forehead with the back of her hand and tried to imagine a double vodka, nice and cold.

She was glancing down at her heel, looking for blood, when a brown bird, the size of a large rooster, flew in front of her and landed on the road, blocking the way. The bird flapped its speckled wings menacingly.

Meredith froze, returning the bird's beady stare.

"A guinea hen," Henry whispered from behind. "Don't move. She might attack. She's probably protecting her nest."

"What...should...I...do...?" Meredith said under her breath, her throat dry. She looked at the wild creature tripling its size with its wingspan. Was the thing deadly? Its beak was long and undoubtedly sharp. She recalled Hitchcock's *The Birds*. Did birds really do things like attack humans? *How did she get here?*

Henry touched her arm lightly and took her hand. "She's probably nesting nearby and could be vicious. When I say *go*, follow me closely."

Meredith watched the hen, waiting.

"Go!" Henry pulled her through the grass, circling around the bird, making smooth strides, quietly covering ground.

But Meredith's foot hit a boulder. She lost Henry's grip and flew forward. Arms outstretched, she slid into the grass.

She looked up. A few feet away, the hen stared at her, eye level. Henry waited on the other side of the clearing, safe. The bird's feathers ruffled, and she cocked her head with unblinking eyes. The top feather rose erect, like an antenna.

"Oh no," Meredith whispered. She cooed in her softest voice, "Nice hen, nice hen, it's all right. I won't hurt you." Slowly, she raised herself up. A searing pain shot through her hip.

Henry was making strange noises, bird calls, she thought. He waved his hat. Meredith realized he was creating a distraction.

The hen turned toward his cries.

Meredith dragged her bad leg to the path, limped to the other side of the clearing, and collapsed on a log next to Henry. Her face throbbed, but the bandage had remained in place. She trembled.

"Henry," she sobbed, "this is too much. I'm hot and tired and dirty, and I've hurt my hip. I can't walk and my face hurts.... You've got to go and get help...."

"I don't think so," he said with a slight smile. He sat beside her, checked her face and leg, and put his arm around her. "You'll be fine. It was just a guinea hen. Nothing's bleeding. Come along."

With his arm around her waist, she hobbled alongside, down the long dusty road with its ruts and weeds, through more pastures and forest, and finally to the highway and the car.

How glad she was she hadn't cancelled that flight home. *This place is a nightmare.*

⌘ ⌘ ⌘

Meredith cleaned up as best she could, sipping a vodka Henry carried upstairs and rubbing Nani's herbal cream onto her bruised hip. She asked for second helpings at dinner and Nani beamed her gummy grin, then waddled into the kitchen to retrieve more white fish crusted with macadamias, warm taro rolls, and purple sweet potatoes mashed with honey and butter. There were leafy greens from the garden, and small yellow tomatoes. Lucy listened to her father's account of the day's adventures and showed him a new kite Sammy had given her. Meredith ate as though it were her last meal on earth.

After dinner, as they sat in the library holding large snifters of rum, she nearly forgot the pain, the humiliation, of the afternoon. Making love by the falls seemed long ago as she listened to the soothing patter of rain on the porch roof. It was a warm rain and the windows were partially open, though the drapes remained closed. Nani and Lucy sat in the wicker rocker brought in from the verandah and the old tutu was beginning a story. Henry smoked a pipe, sending curls into the air, glancing occasionally at Meredith, then at his daughter, his book open and unread on his lap. The moment was sweet, sweet like the musky smell of the smoke, sweet like Henry's gaze upon the old woman and child. His eyes held the past, as though he saw someone else, maybe Maria. Meredith stood outside the moment, looking in, and glimpsed something precious.

She fingered the book Henry had given her to read. "The beginning of your education," he said. She would play along, for to her surprise, their conversations had been entertaining, something different, something new. No one in her world spoke as he did. It was like a game, a word game, or maybe an idea game, where their phrases met and wove and parried, challenging and connecting, creating thoughts and merging into ideas. Rather like exercise, she thought, only using mental muscles, flexing cranial tendons. It was fun. If the brain had abs or glutes, why not work them out a bit?

"And so, Lucy," Nani was saying as they rocked in the chair, "our family goes back and back and back to the early Hawaiians who came to these islands in their outriggers and settled the land. They fished and planted and cared for one another."

Meredith glanced at Henry and he smiled, then turned his eyes again on his daughter. He seemed strangely content.

"They sing and dance too." Lucy nodded and wiggled into Nani's side. "Don't forget, they sing and dance, Tutu Nani."

"Yes," Nani replied, "they sing and dance their stories."

"Why, Nani?"

"To show their love."

"To show their love?"

Meredith steadied her glass on her open book and watched them. She hadn't spent much time with her own grandparents. Her mother's parents had died in a car crash before she was born. Her father never spoke of *his* father, as if the subject was off limits, and she had assumed some terrible story of jail or abuse, but never knew. Then there was Granny Lynne, her father's mother.

Her memories of Granny Lynne were early and few. She remembered crawling on a stool to stir oats into cookie batter, watched by the jolly Quaker on the red cardboard canister. She recalled tea with milk and toast strips for dunking. And there was a red spaniel, Freckles, who ate with his ears clothes-pinned above his head to keep them out of his food. He didn't seem to mind. When her parents divorced, she saw less and less of Granny Lynne. Now, as she watched Nani, she wondered what had become of her.

Nani's voice floated in the air, soothing and rhythmic, like a slow dance. "The stories tell how they work hard. They grow food and catch fish for their families. This shows their love. They care for their children. This shows their love. They are brave and fight for their people. This shows their love. They make laws to govern their people.

This shows their love."

"What is *gover?*"

"Gover*n* means they teach their people what is good and bad, right and wrong."

"What is *good?*" Lucy asked.

Henry and Meredith exchanged glances. They looked at Nani.

Nani smiled. "She's a wise one, Henry, a wise one she is." She tapped her nose.

Henry nodded.

"That's another story for another night," Nani said to Lucy.

"Lucy," Henry said, *"good* is *love."*

"And *God* is love," Nani said. "Some people run away from love. That is not good. That makes God sad."

"Where do they go?"

"They do not know."

"Why?"

"Another story for another night, Lucy."

"Oh." The child folded her hands in her lap with resignation.

"Now, little one, it is time for bed and old Nani is going to bed too." Nani lifted herself from the chair and took Lucy's hand.

They paused in the doorway and Nani turned.

"You coming, Henry? Coming to kiss Lucy good night?"

"I'll be right there." He stood, set down his empty glass and book, and kissed Meredith lightly on the forehead.

Meredith watched them leave. She was on the edge of a dream, a wonderful dream, but she couldn't find her way inside. She thought of their day in the jungle, of Henry and Nani and Lucy. Hana-lani was not her home. She didn't belong in this Hawaiian outback. Her home, what was left of it, was San Francisco, where people did things, went places, *shopped.* They were fashionable and wore nice things. They ate in trendy restaurants and saw Broadway shows on Geary Street. They talked about *real* stuff, guys and jobs and vacations. They didn't wander in the wilds and meet up with dangerous birds.

She touched her face. The bandages were still in place and her skin still tender. She definitely needed more time to heal.

Meredith stood and walked to the narrow opening in the draperies.

Peering into the dark sky, she feared her own soul was like that black universe, vast and empty. She felt a sudden chill.

Eighteen

The week passed, and Meredith looked forward to her time with the child, although she wouldn't admit it. Lucy was sounding out words, and soon, Meredith sensed, would be reading sentences. She practiced letters with her pencil on her ruled newsprint tablet, waiting for Meredith to approve or disapprove.

The days fell into a pleasant routine. Breakfast at the long table. Lessons with Lucy, lunch, play with Lucy, sometimes by the tide pools with Nani and the dogs. Tea and cocktails in the afternoon in the library or on the verandah. After dinner, more reading time with Lucy.

Later, she climbed the stairs to the deep feather bed. Soon Henry joined her. He turned out to be a thoughtful lover, slow and sensitive, holding back. She feared he was becoming a habit that would be difficult to break.

She mentioned the Debate Club and gave Henry the flyer as she had promised Sammy. Henry had grown sad. "Not a bad idea one day. But not just yet. I need my privacy." But he called Sammy, reaching for the phone with apparent determination and inviting him to go jogging or play a little ball the next time he was in Hana. A surprising relief poured through Meredith that their distance had been bridged. Why should she care?

She finished the book Henry had lent her, and began another, Paul Johnson's *Modern Times*, much thicker. She doubted she'd get through that one, but holding the book and working through a few pages at a time gave her a sense of accomplishment, as though her life were moving in an orderly direction. Henry gave her index cards to jot down questions and quotes she liked.

The skies would open and the rain would pour. Just as suddenly, the trade winds blew the clouds up the mountain, clearing the heavy humidity. She watched the skies and the forests and the grasslands, and she watched Nani and Henry. She turned down a path filled with color and sweetness, led by a young child, a middle aged man, and an old woman.

Friday afternoon, Meredith and Lucy knocked on Henry's study door.

"You promised another outing, Henry," Meredith said from the hallway.

His voice was muffled. "Er...right.... Just a sec." The door opened. His eyes were red and watery.

Meredith smiled. "Not getting enough...sleep?" she asked coyly.

Lucy grabbed his leg. "You promised! You promised! We're going to the little church!"

A church?

"Lindbergh's grave. I completely forgot. Give me ten minutes. I'm writing, Meredith! It's coming together at last." He shook his head in amazement. "But a promise is a promise, isn't it, Lucy? What's a broken promise, Lucy? What did I tell you?"

"A broken promise is a broken trust."

"And what is a broken trust?"

"A broken trust is a broken heart."

"Very good."

Meredith breathed deeply. "Ready in fifteen minutes?"

"Right, darling." He kissed her lightly.

She bristled. A married person's word, an implied contract. They had no contract.

But now they were going to a church and a grave. What happened to waterfalls and beaches?

Her flight was still scheduled for Wednesday, and it was for the best.

⌘⌘⌘

Henry turned the car onto a shady dirt road. "It's right up here. The Palapala Ho'omau Church."

They drove through the forest and into a clearing. A white chapel with a brown pitched roof and a small cupola stood in a quiet garden. A steppingstone path led to a red door and white portico. At the entrance to the path a weathered wooden sign read:

> You are welcome to enter this church in a spirit of reverence
> befitting any place of worship. Those who wish to walk quietly
> on the surrounding paths are asked not to step on the graves
> or disturb stones or flowers out of respect for the deceased
> and consideration for the feelings of the relatives.

Lucy raced ahead and waited on the porch, her fuchsia sundress brilliant against the white paint.

"Come, come," she cried. "Come into the little church."

The door was open. Inside, green painted benches faced a raised platform, and a simple wooden cross stood at the far end. A white podium in the left corner was angled toward the empty pews.

"It's Congregational," Henry said. "That's why it's so plain. The Congregationalists were influenced by the Puritans."

"Oh." Meredith checked her nails, unpolished and ragged, and frowned.

"The Puritans feared images," he was saying, "kind of dreary, to my way of thinking."

"I thought you didn't believe in those things."

Lucy wandered toward the cross.

"Lucy, come back," Henry called. He turned to Meredith. "I don't. Where's her headband?"

"She must have left it in the van. So, if you don't believe, what difference does it make?"

"None really. It's merely space others think sacred." He sounded wistful.

"It's clean."

"That's the idea, purging false worship. The Reformers actually used the imagery of pollution; they felt that prayers to saints, particularly to Mary, and veneration of images polluted churches with false belief. You remember the Ten Commandments, the commandment about worshiping graven images."

The heat in the enclosed space was suffocating, and Meredith wondered why the Puritans should matter to her anyway.

Lucy skipped down the aisle toward them. She grabbed their hands and pulled them toward the door. "Let's go to the garden and see the kitties."

"Last time we found feral cats in the bushes," Henry explained.

They walked outside to the cemetery behind the church. Henry paused before a plaque resting on a bed of river rock where flowers, tied in a ribbon, had been left. A small American flag rose in the grass.

"The flowers are *Bird of Paradise*," Henry said as he watched Lucy run between the plumeria trees.

"They're incredible." The blossoms, with their long necks and bright orange topknots, did indeed look like birds.

Henry pointed to the plaque. "Here's his grave."

CHARLES A. LINDBERGH
BORN MICHIGAN 1902 DIED MAUI 1974

*"...If I take the wings of the morning,
and dwell in the uttermost parts of the sea..."*
C.A.L.

Henry rubbed his beard. "According to Nani, Lindbergh didn't write that, but it must have been a favorite quote. It's from the Psalms."

The name *Lindbergh* was familiar, but Meredith couldn't recall who he was. Maybe he was a soldier, since there was a flag, she thought. Would Henry think her a dimwit if she asked who he was? She watched him for a hint.

They walked out to the edge of the garden where the sea pounded the cliffs.

"He died of cancer in 1974, here in Hana. He designed his own grave and coffin."

"Kind of morbid."

Henry glanced at her. "Realistic, I would say. You *do* know who he was, don't you?"

"Of course."

"He was a great American."

"He was."

"We wouldn't be here in Hawaii if it weren't for him."

"No." *Think, Meredith, think.*

"What do you suppose his greatest achievement was?"

"Uh...well.... He was so *patriotic*."

"You *don't* know who he was, *do* you?"

Meredith shook her head. "Henry, what difference does it make? He's *dead*. You're so arrogant." She bit her lip.

Henry frowned and turned abruptly. He walked toward Lucy, who had crawled into some bushes on the far side of the lawn, and called to her. She emerged from the foliage, and he took her hand. They headed back to the car.

"Where are the kitties, Papa?" Lucy whined.

Meredith groaned as she followed them. *Strike one.* She had a good thing going. She didn't need to cut him off yet. She caught up with them.

"Have you no sense of history?" he said as he turned the key in the ignition. "How it affects our lives? Our thoughts? Our presuppositions?"

Presuppositions? "I'm sorry, Henry, I guess not. Maybe you could teach me. I *am* reading the books you loaned me." She tried to keep the anger out of her voice and to sound as helpless as possible. How was she supposed to know who Lindbergh was? And what were presuppositions?

He sighed. "*I* should be the one who's sorry. You're young and intelligent, but I expect too much."

"So, who *was* Lindbergh?" She wasn't that uneducated. She had a college degree.

"Charles Lindbergh was a pioneering aviator. He flew the first solo flight across the Atlantic, nonstop from New York to Paris."

"Really?" He had a lot of guts, she thought.

"And during his life he did a lot to promote aviation and open routes for jet travel."

"Now *that* I can appreciate."

Henry grew thoughtful. "But his life was marked by tragedy as well. His little boy was kidnapped and murdered."

"How awful." She glanced at Lucy stretched out on the back seat, asleep, her thumb in her mouth, her headband clutched in her other hand. Lucy's thick black lashes fluttered. She was dreaming.

"And he campaigned for America to stay out of the war against Hitler. He was considered by many to be a Nazi sympathizer. I'd say he was simply misguided. Many well-intentioned people were taken in by the propaganda in those days. They didn't believe the reports of concentration camps. Even so, Lindbergh was a public figure and influential."

"Like Hollywood stars taking sides?"

He smiled. "You catch on quickly."

"As though money gives you the right to be an expert."

"Exactly. Money and fame do not equal expertise."

"It was beautiful there, in the cemetery, not spooky at all. I've never been to a cemetery before."

"You're kidding. Sorry, I'm sounding arrogant again."

"Couldn't see any point in it." She refused to go with her mother to visit her grandparents' graves each year. It seemed too weird, and she always found something better to do.

Henry drove in silence, taking each bend in the road carefully, and Meredith sensed he was forming another explanation. As she waited, she inhaled the sweet floral scents through the car window and watched the play of the sun on her arm. Her tan had definitely improved.

"Most of us," he said, as he turned up the gravel drive to Hana-lani, "don't think about death. Avoiding the subject is a built-in mechanism to shield us from despair. Nevertheless, it's good to be reminded. And graveyards do that. They remind us of death and in that way help us understand life. *In my beginning is my end.* T.S. Eliot. We are born to die."

Meredith shuddered. "How does death help us understand life, Henry?"

"The graves remind us that our days are numbered and thus encourage effective use of those days. Most important, they ask one of the larger questions, the permanent questions."

"The questions again?"

"The graves ask, *What happens when we die?*"

"And how do you answer the question of the graves?"

He pulled up to the house and turned off the motor. Looking into her eyes, he ran his hand down her hair, released the golden waves from their wide silk band, and arranged them over her shoulders. His touch was pleasing, like a gentle breeze, like Lucy's touch but firmer and with greater intent.

"I don't have the answer," he said. "Nani does; the Christians do; the Buddhists and Hindus do as well. All I can say is that it's certain we will die, and it's good to recall that."

He sounded so sad, confronted with this obvious fact.

"Then we must make effective use of our days." She smiled her broadest smile and lowered her lids provocatively.

"The most effective use." He leaned toward her lips.

Nineteen

Nani had bad days and good days.

Her fingers were swollen with arthritis, and her lower back often ached. The veins in her legs bulged, and she walked with a limp from long-ago foot surgery. Sammy had warned her about her heart and her lack of exercise, but she had laughed him off. "I got too much to do to exercise," she told him, and the minor stroke ten years ago had been no surprise. Since then she had lost fifty pounds. She had eaten less poi and taken up dancing.

She cut back on her groups—making layettes for newborns, singing in the choir, baking for the church bazaars, helping at the Senior Center. Instead of organizing, she took to advising, tutoring her replacements, and becoming honorary this and honorary that, lifetime this and lifetime that, emeritus of everything, it seemed. All of Hana were her children, and they would never let her be, happy as they were to hold onto her apron strings.

On Nani's good days, when her sleepiness and pain did not take over, she visited her circles of friends. She helped with the quilting when her fingers allowed, but often she simply watched, humming softly, and dozing for a bit. She might shuffle into the kitchen to oversee the making of tea. She listened to her grown children, now grandparents, chatter about their worries and their loves, their hopes and their fears, as she nodded her double chin or shook her head. "Let Tutu Nani-lei decide," one would say, and they would all look to her.

The children played in the yard, running and screaming, and heading for the covered porch when a sudden rain fell from the heavens. She could stop them with a look, and did, once and again, just to remind them they weren't in charge. She told them stories of Jesus when she could, for those were her favorite, and she knew some children would listen and some wouldn't. Some would believe and some wouldn't. That's just the way it was.

Nani's faith centered on the whalebone cross she wore on her leathery skin. It centered too on the wooden cross in the white sanctuary of Wananalua Congregational Church, established 1838. The cross made Nani happy. It gave meaning to her life, structure to her family, and answers to her questions. When Willie died, and went to be with Maria and Bets and Jimmy and Keoko and sweet Lou, she knew the parting was only temporary, as if they were on vacation. One day soon she would join them and all the others she had seen off, waving from the shore. Some days she wished it was her turn to be seen off. She missed them, and she was so very sleepy.

In her younger days, when she had an hour off work, she liked to walk up the mountain, through the green pasturelands dotted with Mr. Fagan's cows, up the steep path to the giant lava cross Mrs. Fagan built when he died. She would arrive out of breath, holding her skirts, and would touch the rough stone of the cross. Looking out over the coast, north to Keanae and south to Hamoa Bay, with Hana, the settlement of her birth, nesting nicely in between, she could see her own church, which Henry's daddy once pastored, on a corner near the ranch. Across the highway stood the Catholic church, begun by missionaries from far away and today mostly Filipino. To the south, downtown Hana covered two blocks, if that, with its post office, bank, grill, and gas station. Hasegawa's had taken over the old theater, where she and Lou held hands for the first time, and he had nervously kissed her on the cheek. What a rush she had with that kiss! She often grew warm thinking about it. Beyond the ranch, the one-room school held classes she never attended, needed as she was in the fields, but later she sat in a circle with the *keikis*, making leis and telling her stories and leading them in the dance.

When Nani looked over Hana from the heights of Fagan's Cross, she could spot Rose's shed and Daniel's vegetable garden and the chimney the men repaired last winter after the bad storm. Surely she had carried lunch to every field at one time or other as her boys had moved from place to place. She could see in her mind the horse that got loose, running like the wind down the coast. From that hillside, Nani had watched for Lou's return from the north, checking for the flag he raised over his berth in the inlet where he moored. He knew all the best spots, Lou did, and taught them to their sons, and she would count the coves and bays and figure herself a lucky woman to have such a husband as that Lou Brown. Finally, beyond the fish ponds, stood Hana-lani, a house that grew with each generation, up and out, on and on, a white cathedral of a home surrounded by green fields.

Nani's eye would return to Kauiki Head, beyond the ranch and the school, a rocky lava promontory that had once boiled into the sea and now rose peacefully in blue waters, crowned with foliage, and she would thank God for its lighthouse that warned the fishermen in bad weather. She would thank God for other blessings too, her life, her family, her faith. She would gaze between the arm and the foot of the huge cross, over the coastland, and pray for whatever needed praying for—Joe's job, Annie's baby, Mindy's infertility, Max's drinking; sins of pride, covetousness, envy, hatred, sloth, gluttony, lust. She prayed for the children in the school that they'd get things sorted out, and she prayed for her parents who seemed to be always fighting. When she was done, she listened for Jesus' voice and her heart most times grew warm, beating hard. Sometimes she cried, but most times she laughed, and up there, on the side of the mountain with the clouds gathering on the peak and the haze moving up from the sea below, the green grasslands open before her, no one cared how loud or how long she laughed or cried. Those were her young to middle years, and as her aging body confined her to flat ground, she sought moments to gaze on Fagan's cross, its silhouette strong and beckoning against the green mountain, and talked to Jesus just the same from wherever she was.

Lately, she had dreamed of the cross on the hillside. It seemed to call her, and as she woke she held onto the sweetness, for she could smell roses and jasmine, and trade winds lifted her up. She glided, weightless.

⌘ ⌘ ⌘

Sunday morning Tutu Nani-lei sat in the second pew of Wananalua Congregational, Lucy on one side and old Hodgson, chewing tobacco and tapping his foot, on the other. "Hush," she said into his good ear and pointing to his thick toes protruding from rubber sandals.

Nani gazed at the giant white cross that rose between the flags of her country and her state, commanding the center of the chancel. She liked the clean white of the walls, the plainness. The mahogany pews lining the burgundy-carpeted aisle were a heavy contrast to the white, as though they rooted the people, kept them from floating away in such an airy place. The church elders, along with Pastor Kanuki, sat in chairs on a broad white dais, three steps up, behind a holy table used for communion once a month. Looking from that dark nave to that white chancel was like looking from earth to heaven, Nani often thought. Her eye focused on the large brass baptismal bowl to the side of the holy table. Soon it would be used for little Lucy Maria. She prayed she would live to see it.

The preacher had spoken his words, words to explain the Word of God, the Word made flesh, a kind of manna, he said. "God sent manna to the People of Israel to feed them in the desert," he concluded as he looked over his flock, "and he gave his Son to us, the Word of God, to be our manna to feed us in the desert of this life."

Nani smiled. Pastor Kanuki had explained to her once that this *manna* was different from the *mana* of old Hawaii, the spiritual power passed on through their chiefs, but his arguments didn't convince her. "The roots of the words are different," Pastor Kanuki said. "One is Hebrew and one is Maori."

Nani tapped her nose and sighed. She believed they came from the same place, and he just didn't get it. Maybe she didn't read and maybe she didn't have much education, but how do they know the Maori word and the Hebrew word didn't come from something even earlier? How did they know that, anyway? That was just too much of a coincidence to believe otherwise. And Nani believed true coincidences were rare.

Pastor Fitzhugh, Henry's daddy, wouldn't have said such silly things, although she didn't recall his position on *mana* and *manna*. He was a good pastor, a caring pastor, but to leave Henry in order to preach far away was hard on the boy, especially since Henry was an only child and a quiet one at that. Growing up in Hana, he had been different from the other haoles who surfed the waters off Hamoa Bay and hiked the trails to the falls. He preferred his books to the outdoors even then, skipped a grade in school, and spent long hours in the Hana library.

"He brings home ten books at a time," his mother would say at the coffee hour after church, "and works his way through them. He'd bring home more, but that's the limit."

Pastor Fitzhugh would wrap his arm around his wife and chuckle proudly. "He's very bright, our boy is, Henry's very bright."

Nani welcomed Henry to Hana-lani and smothered him with love as best she could, and even more love when his folks passed on to heaven. She took care of Pastor Fitzhugh's boy, she did.

The hymn was announced, and Nani grabbed the pew-back and pulled herself up with both hands. Lucy stood too and hummed along. Pastor Fitzhugh and Mrs. Fitzhugh, God rest their souls, would have loved little Lucy…how they would have loved her.

O worship the King, all glorious above!
O gratefully sing his power and his love!
Our shield and defender, the Ancient of Days,
Pavilioned in splendor, and girded with praise.

Nani sang the words by heart, belting her deep contralto to the cross, feeling the child clutching her skirts. It was the last hymn, the one when the black-robed preacher processed out, and it was her last chance with the cross for that week. She gazed at it, as she usually did, memorizing its lines and waiting for an answer she could keep in her heart, holding her palms together as she had been taught so long ago. *Dear Jesus, if she is the one for Henry, let her stay and heal him. You know it's almost my time to come home to you. They say you are the Ancient of Days and you have power and love. Then, dear Lord, I give you my worries. Here they are, take them all.*

With a lighter heart, Nani took Lucy's hand and followed the crowd out slowly, never sure if she would see that cross again, at least on this earth. She lingered, looking up the aisle once more.

She turned to the others in line, chatting to some and hugging others, checking on the problems she had prayed for the past week, till she got to Pastor Kanuki. She shook his hand, thinking the robe he wore must be warm today. She grinned as though they shared a private joke and looked about for Henry and the girl.

They were to join her at the gravesite, Maria's gravesite, to honor the second anniversary of her granddaughter's death.

She led Lucy to the cemetery to the side of the white stucco church, where stones and plaques stood amidst red ginger and laua'e ferns and neatly mown grass, bordered by yellow hibiscus waving in the breeze. Far beyond the broad lawn, sloping gently, the bright sea crashed against the dark cliffs, and Nani thought of her granddaughter and her love and her early death. Would Maria approve of Henry's choice? She wasn't sure she would.

Henry appeared, Meredith at his side, with the dogs. Eli and Alabar nuzzled Nani's thick hand, hoping for treats, but, finding none, lay at her feet. Lucy crawled on top of Eli and laid her face against his sleek chestnut coat.

"How was church?" Henry asked.

"Good, Henry, good, as always, wish you would join me now and again."

"Sure, Tutu Nani, I will one of these days."

Meredith looked from Nani to Henry and back to Nani. She knelt and stroked Alabar. Nani could see the girl was nervous. It was probably the graves. Some folk didn't understand them.

"Shall we begin?" Henry said.

"Did you bring the lilies?" Nani asked.

He pointed to the fresh flowers at the base of the simple gravestone. Nani studied the letters, recalling their meaning, and mouthing the words to herself.

MARIA ELIZABETH BROWN FITZHUGH
1953—2002
Love Never Dies

They stood around the grassy grave, and in her mind Nani saw Maria's funeral, the dancing, the pastor's comforting words. It had threatened to rain but held off, and the sun beamed upon them as they sang the last hymn.

Nani glanced at Meredith and motioned to Lucy to stand and take her hand.

"Dear Maria," Nani said, her eyes closed, "we will never forget you and will always love you. May God grant you peace. We carry your memory in our hearts." She looked at Henry.

He glanced at Meredith. "In our hearts," he mumbled, fidgeting with his ring.

"And we'll see you in heaven, Mama." Lucy touched the gravestone and placed a plumeria blossom on top of the lilies.

"Amen," Nani said and clasped her palms together.

Henry stared at the grass. "Amen," he murmured.

"Amen," Lucy said, looking up at Nani.

Meredith whispered something under her breath.

Nani turned to Meredith. "Henry, take Lucy. I want to talk to Miss Campbell for a minute."

She motioned to the young woman to follow her to the edge of the grassy knoll.

"You're not a believer," Nani said, "are you, Meredith?"

Meredith looked away. "No, I'm sorry, Nani, I'm not."

Nani studied the beautiful, damaged face. Her cuts were healing with the herbal ointments and the girl's youth, but the scars would be a reminder for some time. Her eyes were cornflower blue and her hair an amber blond rarely seen in Hana. It hung in unreal waves down her back.

"I'm sorry as well," Nani said, "but maybe it's better that way. Henry doesn't believe either. If he married a believer, he would break her heart."

"Married a believer?" Meredith nervously twisted a strand of hair.

"Meredith, what exactly are your intentions?" Nani rested her hand on the girl's smooth arm, hoping she would turn and face her.

"My intentions?" Meredith continued to look away.

"With regard to my grandson, my grandson-in-law, that is."

"I'm not sure what you mean."

"He loves you. You know that, don't you, child?" Nani placed her hands on her hips and moved around to face her.

"Well...." Meredith looked up toward the mountain.

"Do you love *him?*"

Meredith raised her hands. *"God*, Nani..."

"Be praised. Well?"

"I...I guess so."

"Oh, sweet Jesus." Nani turned abruptly and pulled herself up the hill toward Lucy and Henry. "What a pickle we have here. Come along, young lady, come along." Then, suddenly, Tutu Nani stopped and turned on her heel. "Miss Campbell, don't play my grandson along. Be honest. Can you do that? His heart is broke already. He doesn't need the pieces stomped on and scattered to the four winds."

She threw her thick hands in the air, picked up her skirts, and headed back up the hill, watching for uneven patches and shaking her head. "Oh, sweet Jesus, sweet Jesus, help us now," she cried, looking up to the white church with its tall steeple and beyond, to Fagan's cross against the mountain.

Twenty

"You've got to stay out of this, Nani," Henry warned. He reached for a towel to dry the dishes his grandmother was washing.

He wasn't sure what Nani and Meredith had spoken about earlier, but he could see the two weren't speaking now. Sunday lunch had been awkward, to say the least. He guessed Nani had embarrassed Meredith, probably asked her what her intentions were. His tutu was famous for that. She had meddled in nearly everyone's affairs, if they involved one of her own. She was a jealous mother hen looking out for her loved ones. He had to admit she was usually right.

Meredith and Lucy had escaped the tension-filled room to feed the dogs on the back stoop.

"She's no good, Henry; she'll break your heart all over." Nani handed him a pot to dry and plunged her hands into the sudsy water. He had offered to buy her a dishwasher, but she had refused.

"You needn't worry, Nani. I'm okay."

"She'll be on that plane on Wednesday, Henry, three days from now. You'll see."

"She's staying on. She told me so."

Nani whistled through her teeth and stared out the kitchen window into her garden as though the end of the world were upon them.

She turned and eyed him with her piercing gaze. "Henry, be careful, okay?" It was the gaze she used when he had taken Maria to the falls, to the beach, and up the mountain, unchaperoned. "What are your intentions?" she had asked him then. Her question had forced him to think about an answer.

"Nani, you worry too much." He lifted a plate, set it on the towel over his palm, wiped one side dry, then the other, and placed it on the stack in the cupboard. The pungent garden mint, growing under the window, mingled with the fading aromas of roast pork and ginger. He didn't recall those aromas, in that enticing combination.

Henry knew he was in deep, but he was enjoying it. His choices were few, his path clear. He would spend eternity with this creature if she would have him, and he didn't care what the terms were. He inhaled the fragrant air and reached for another plate. Nani stared at the sudsy water, stone-faced, mechanically washing and rinsing, washing and rinsing. The dishes were piling up in the rubber drainer faster than he could dry them.

Maria would be pleased that he was among the living again. Meredith had opened his eyes, long clamped shut, and had revived his heart, long numb. He noticed things now: aromas carried on delicate breezes, sounds of waves pounding upon rocks, birds singing at dawn and dusk. He saw the blues of the sea and sky, the greens of the forests and pastures, the yellows and corals of the plumeria and hibiscus, the red earth and the black rock, the amber sand. All of Hana was a Matisse canvas, Chagall stained glass. Through the kitchen window, Haleakala loomed above its verdant flanks, jutting into the cerulean sky. He placed another dried plate on the stack, lining up the rims of orange and yellow.

But most of all, he noticed Lucy and how she needed him. How could he have abandoned her at such a time? Maria would have frowned, her arms folded, her feet planted firmly on the ground, flat-footed. A sense of righteous purpose flooded him, for now when he watched his daughter's face he noticed expressions of interest, hope, or boredom. When had her hearing last been checked? Surely they could ready her for school. There must be a tutor for things like that. He would see to it. The image of his selfishness, a narcissistic contentment fed by rum and isolation, accused him, again and again. Meredith had changed all that. She had healed him, or begun the healing. Could he close his eyes even if he wanted to? Could he halt the healing? He had forgotten what life was all about. Life was love, and love was life, as trite as it sounded. It took simple Meredith to show him that, and he was grateful.

"You just be careful, my boy," Nani repeated. She scrubbed as though purging demons. She turned the faucet high, deluging the pans.

Henry shook his head, not understanding her. Why wasn't she happy for him after all this time?

And Meredith, after all, wasn't that simple. She had a sharp mind, simply undeveloped. He would tutor her, bring her lovingly along, and they would be closer than ever. She would learn about love and suffering, love and sacrifice. Why, she was learning already, he was sure of it from their conversations so far. He dried a pot and hung it on a hook.

He was beginning to think again: to analyze, dissect, and plan. His mind, as though awakened from a coma, had sharpened, and he had made significant progress with the manuscript. He would read to Meredith what he had written so far. He would ask her opinion.

She got on well with Lucy, Henry thought, reaching for a soapy rag and wiping the counter down, and with Nani too, for the most part. Maybe Meredith would want children of her own. He could see Lucy as big sister, shepherding, organizing. Would their children be dark or fair? Girls or boys? What would they name them?

He folded his towel and hung it neatly on the rod under the sink. "Why would she lie about staying, Nani?"

Nani shook her head and shuffled toward the back stoop.

"Lucy," she called, "let's go look at the tide pools. Old Nani needs some fresh air, that's for sure. This house is too stale for old Tutu."

He wouldn't let Nani spoil things. He would show her how wrong she was. He looked at his ring, pulled it off, and slipped it in his shirt pocket. He found Meredith on the verandah chaise.

"Come, darling," he said. "Let's walk."

She took his hand, her brows raised, her eyes questioning.

Below the horizon, the ocean shimmered in silvers and grays under a dark cloudbank, but farther down the coast, the waters graduated to deep blues.

He led Meredith through the grass down to the cliffs, feeling her long fine-boned fingers, protected by his. How good it was to care for someone again, and he savored the connection, so delicate, so powerful. When had he last held hands with a woman? He was sixteen again, walking with Maria, her skirts billowing.

Meredith's flowered pareo and turquoise jersey outlined her body, a slim but not-too-slim body, Henry thought. His blood raced as he glanced at her form so close by, the full bosom, the narrow waist. She matched his pace as they stepped toward the sea, her hips sliding rhythmically. The wind lifted her loose hair high. She was a creature from another world. Henry's heart thundered.

They paused on the edge of the cliff. The rough sea sent whitecaps flying and cobalt swells rolled powerfully toward the shore.

"This is my favorite place," he said as he recalled his wedding vows. The hau tree stood nearby like an eternal presence, watching him map his future.

"It's beautiful." Her voice choked. "You can see way up the coast."

"I'm sorry. The plane went down near here. How thoughtless of me."

"No problem. I'm past that now." She touched her bandages and looked up at him, her brows furrowed, her thoughts hidden behind large dark glasses.

"Meredith," he began. "You've brought me back to life, you know." He traced her good cheek with his finger and slipped a golden strand of hair behind her ear.

"I think you did that yourself, mister." She grinned.

"We did it together."

"Let's visit the tide pools." She grabbed his hand. "Lucy and Nani are down there with the dogs."

"Wait. I want to say something, something private."

His hand shook as he pulled from his pants pocket a tiny box made from minute shells. The afternoon light glimmered on the layered opalescence.

"We really should go," she said, a touch of fear in her voice.

Henry knelt in the grass and spoke his rehearsed words to the turquoise flowers swirling up her body. "Meredith, will you save me from myself? From my loneliness? Will you marry me? I love you, and I know you love me." He looked up.

Her face was turned toward the sea. "Henry –"

He swallowed hard. "You don't have to answer now."

"Henry...you don't understand, do you?" She continued to look away.

"You don't have to answer now," he said again, filled with foreboding. He rose and reached for her shoulder, turning her toward him. He removed her glasses and searched her eyes, so blue. *Like the sea on a sunny day.* He touched her hair. *Like silk, corn silk. Baby fine.*

Her eyes were troubled. This was not going well.

"I'm sorry, Henry, I can't marry you." She turned and headed for the house.

"Just think about it?" he called after her.

"There's nothing to think about," she shouted back.

Henry stood on the promontory and watched her leave, her stride determined. Why? What had he misread? He was too old, he supposed. Too old and too foolish. His heart ached.

Nani looked up from the tide pools and waved. He climbed down to join them, shifting his mind to another sphere as he tried to mask the pain.

"What have you got there, Lucy?" he asked, his smile forced.

Her refusal must not shove him back into the dark. Not again. He wouldn't allow it. *But what a fool he was.*

⌘ ⌘ ⌘

Henry didn't visit Meredith that night. Breakfast was strained and silent. Lucy's wide eyes moved from face to face as she sucked her thumb and swung her legs against the chair rungs. Meredith had withdrawn into herself. Even Nani had no words.

Finally, Henry threw his napkin on the table and stood. "Let's go somewhere for the day, all of us. Meredith leaves the day after next, right, Ms. Meredith?" He tried to sound cheerful.

"The princess is leaving us?" Lucy wailed. She jumped off her chair and leaned against Meredith, looking up at her and petting her arm. "Please don't go."

"Ms. Campbell needs to return home," Henry explained to Lucy, "to San Francisco. She has places to go, people to see...." He darted a glance at Meredith. She seemed to wince.

"I'm sorry." Meredith put an arm around Lucy. "I'll miss you."

She seems genuinely upset, Henry thought, *a real good actress.* "So, what do you say, what shall it be?"

"Tsk, tsk." Nani shook her head and rose to clear the table.

"Nani," Henry said, "you decide."

"O Lordy, I suppose we could go down to Hana Bay. Buy lunch at the beach stand. Maybe fly Lucy's new kite."

"We'll have hotdogs!" Lucy cried.

"Eli and Alabar enjoy the pier." Nani carried a stack of dishes into the kitchen. "And it's not far. They say a big storm is coming up from the south. We should stay close to home."

Meredith carried her plate into the kitchen. "I've never been to Hana Bay." She glanced at Henry.

"Then it's decided." The outing would help Henry work through his feelings. *At the same time,* he thought, *she might change her mind.* There was time. "Shall we leave in half an hour?"

"What about your writing?" Meredith asked.

"It can wait."

"What about the permanent things? The great questions?"

"Going to Hana Bay is a permanent thing." He gazed at Lucy thankfully. "Lucy is a permanent thing."

"What is permen?" Lucy asked.

"I'm going to show you." Henry lifted her up on his shoulders and headed down the hall toward her room. "Just as soon as we pack your sweater and bucket and shovel. Where did you put the kite, Lucy?"

She screamed with delight and grabbed his ears, his beard.

He tried not to show the pain.

Twenty-one

Henry, Meredith, and Lucy lunched on hotdogs slathered with relish, mustard, and catsup. Nani slurped a shake. Next to their weathered picnic table on the edge of the beach stood a BEWARE OF UNDERTOW sign. A wind blew over the sea, spraying foam across the sand. A crumbling cement pier jutted into the waters alongside Kauiki Head. Farther out, fishing boats were moored, bobbing on the swells.

Henry and Meredith cleaned up, and Nani spread a quilt in the shade of a *hau* tree as the sun shafted through the moving clouds, burning the earth. Lucy sat next to Nani and waited patiently as her tutu adjusted the headband. Eli stretched out, his head in his paws, and Alabar sat alert.

Nani ran her hand over Lucy's curls. "Did you know, little one, that Queen Kaahumanu was born here in Hana Bay?"

"I know, Nani." Lucy sat cross-legged, her back straight, her hands folded on her lap. She looked toward the rocky peninsula on the other side of the pier. "But tell the story again."

Henry unfolded canvas chairs. Meredith moved hers into the intermittent sun, stretched out her legs, and dug her heels into the sand. She closed her eyes, facing the rays. Henry glanced at Meredith's slim figure. The diamond in her naval sparkled.

"Long ago," Nani crooned, "in a cave on Kauiki Head, a princess was born."

"Kaahumanu!" Lucy cried. "A princess!"

Nani nodded. "Yes, her name was Kaahumanu, and she was beautiful and talented. She was six feet tall with smooth dark skin and big eyes. She liked to surf. She rode the waves better than many men."

"I want to surf, Nani." Lucy pointed to the breaking waves.

Meredith looked up at Lucy, and Henry turned his eyes toward his old tutu. Maybe her words and her love would make everything all right. They had comforted him in the past. They would today.

"You're too little and too young." Nani shook her head and chuckled.

Lucy fiddled with her headband. "What happened next?"

"Is that bothering you?" Nani paused. "Let's take it off for the story, and I'll speak into your ear, little one."

Lucy yanked it off and looked gratefully at Nani. "Okay, ready." She grinned, nodding.

"Let me see it, Lucy." Henry took the band and examined the crocheted pink yarn. Part of the stiff plastic had worn through. That was probably it. He would fix it when they got back.

Nani continued, her face close to Lucy's. "When the princess was sixteen, the great King Kamehameha visited Hana and saw how beautiful she was. And how talented. He asked her to be his queen. She said 'yes' and moved to the Big Island to live with him. All the people loved her."

"Did she throw rocks into Pele's fire too?"

"That was not *her* story. Her story began after the king died." Nani touched the cross on her chest thoughtfully.

"The king died?"

"King Kamehameha died. The queen told her people she would rule with his brother, Lilohilo. Because she had *mana*, holy wisdom, the people agreed."

"*Mana?* Tell what *mana* is again, Tutu. I forget."

"The power of the right words, the wisdom of God."

"Did the queen say the right words?"

"She said, 'No more *kapu* system!' And now the women could eat with the men."

"They could eat bananas." Lucy touched her gum where her new teeth were breaking through, running her finger along the enamel.

"Then, one day, the queen fell ill, and the missionaries prayed for her. She got better, and believed that the missionaries' God had healed her. Their God had great mana, and she wanted that too. So she believed in their God."

"The Lord God Jehovah," said Lucy, nodding.

150

Henry set the headband down. He filled his pipe as he listened to Nani, but he was all too aware of Meredith's presence. How he wished he had some of that mana, whatever it was. How *could* she refuse him? She appeared engrossed with Nani's story, or was she engrossed with Lucy? He tamped the tobacco into the bowl, lit it, drew in deeply, welcoming the spicy burn, and released the smoke into the air. With the smoke, an undefined tension left him as well.

"So," Nani continued, "the queen did the next great thing."

Lucy clapped her hands. "The next great thing!"

Meredith glanced at Henry. Their eyes locked. They looked away.

"The queen ordered her people to learn to read. She set up schools so the missionaries could teach them. She ordered that the Bible be translated into the language of Hawaii. The queen was a Christian, and her people could become Christians too."

"Did the queen learn to read too?"

"She did. She learned in five days. And she made more new laws for her people. Only one wife for one husband. No more drinking too much. No more gambling. No more stealing. No more slaves. No more killing babies. The Ten Commandments said these things were wrong, and the Lord God Jehovah didn't like them."

"*I'm* learning to read," Lucy announced. "My princess is teaching me."

Meredith smiled and glanced at Henry again. He forced a smile, his lips dry against his teeth.

"And," Nani said with a tone of finality, "this great queen was born right here in Hana Bay."

"The End," said Lucy and she clapped her hands together.

"The end of *this* story," said Nani.

"How about flying that kite?" Henry asked. He slipped on his jacket and looked out to the horizon where dark clouds were massing. "It's cooling off, but we have some time before the rain will hit." He pulled out the kite, its dowel cross dividing the tissue into four sections of color: royal blue, emerald green, deep turquoise, and bright coral.

Lucy reached for it and ran her fingers over the thin paper.

"Don't forget Lucy's life vest, Henry," Nani said.

"We're not going in the water. She doesn't need it."

He must remember to teach Lucy to swim. They would begin as soon as the water warmed up a bit and the storms lessened, maybe April.

Lucy and Meredith followed him to the shore, and when he glanced back, Nani had settled herself against the trunk, her hands folded on her lap, her floral muumuu spread out on either side.

Henry carried the kite to the water's edge and let the string unwind a few feet at a time as the wind lifted it up. He handed the string on its plastic holder to Lucy, and she squealed with delight as she ran on the pebbled sand, the kite flapping above her.

The dogs barked and ran alongside. Lucy laughed. Henry took the holder back from Lucy and let the string out farther, then farther, until it was high over the sea.

"Isn't that too far?" Meredith screamed against the wind. "What if it falls into the water?"

"I've got it," Henry shouted back.

"Let me have it, Papa!"

He gave the holder back to Lucy and watched her run with it along the beach, his daughter and the kite skimming the earth. *Maria would have loved this.*

Lucy ran, laughing, pulling the kite toward the pier.

"Lucy, don't go too far...," Henry shouted, running after her. "You don't have your life vest on..."

"Henry!" Meredith cried. "She doesn't have her headband—"

"She can't hear me!" Henry ran. In his panic he could see it all— the dogs loping along with his daughter, urging her, Lucy too far away—and his powerlessness to reach them. He stepped up his pace, his legs like lead.

"Lucy!" he screamed. She was on the pier, pulling the kite, looking up into the sky.

The wind picked up. He could see Alabar skid to a halt at the end of the dock, Eli behind him.

"Lucy!" His voice was drowned in the wind.

Her small form flew over the side.

The dogs paused only seconds and leapt in after her.

Henry reached the edge. Lucy rose to the surface.

"Papa!" she gasped and went under.

He jumped.

It was deep there, at the end of the pier, and the sea sent shock waves through him, his fleece jacket dragging him down. He hit bottom and pushed himself up and saw her form in the green depths. His hand closed on her dress and he pulled her close, kicking wildly to the surface. He emerged, gasping, Lucy limp. The dogs paddled alongside, whining and barking.

He swam, holding her above the water, to the floating boardwalk and lifted her up, handing her to Meredith and the others who had gathered. A siren wailed in the distance.

But the current grabbed his legs, pulling him under and out. He fought to return, to swim upwards, shoving his arms through the water and pushing down, but the shimmering surface drifted farther and farther away....

Finally, he could hold his breath no longer. His lungs screaming, he let the air out slowly, thinking of Maria and Meredith and Nani...and Lucy.... How he loved them all....

Was that music he heard?...one of Nani's hymns...he saw Maria's face, calm and assured, her hands weaving to an old hula tune...beckoning him....

His body was sinking deeper and deeper as he rose above it.... It was no longer his own....

Twenty-two

"**N**o!" Meredith screamed. "Someone go after him!"

"Not in that surf," one of the fishermen said. "Sorry, lady, we can't risk it."

The sea had risen suddenly, angry and thrashing, spilling over the narrow dock.

"I'm taking the dinghy," another man shouted as he jumped into a boat moored to the side. He began to row, but a huge wave sent him back. He tried again but could make no progress.

The paramedics had revived Lucy and wrapped her in blankets. "You'd best tend to the little one," one of them said to Meredith. "Her signs are good. She'll be okay. We'll search for Henry as soon as it's safe."

Meredith lifted the child up and held her close, pressing her soaking head into the hollow of her shoulder.

"Where's Papa?" Lucy sobbed.

"He's coming, Lucy, he's coming soon."

"Where's Nani?"

"Let's find her."

The thought of Nani steadied her panic, and with one last look out to sea, she turned and headed for the beach where the old woman stood, her palms folded, her head raised to the heavens, tears streaming down her weathered skin.

⌘⌘⌘

When Henry did not return and his body was not found, Nani retreated to her room. Numb, Meredith carried trays of pureed vegetables and propped her up on extra pillows. Meredith looked after Lucy.

Sammy came as soon as he heard. He headed a search team up and down the coast. He paced the floors of the old house, making calls and receiving visitors. Meredith was grateful for his steady presence.

Wednesday, the day of her flight, came and went.

"Where's Papa?" Lucy often asked.

"He's gone away for a while." Meredith smoothed the child's long brown curls.

"Will he be gone long?"

"Not long," she said, lying, her throat tight.

"What's wrong with Nani?"

"She's tired and needs to rest."

"Oh."

"Come, let's read a story."

Meredith sat in the wicker rocker. Eli and Alabar settled at her feet. Lucy climbed onto her lap, sucking her thumb.

Meredith opened to the first picture. "This is the story of Peter Pan."

"The boy who could fly."

"Yes, the boy who could fly."

⌘ ⌘ ⌘

Meredith watched Nani sleep. The old woman must be close to death, she thought. Her wrinkled brown skin had creases of gray, and she seemed to have shrunk into the feather pillows and quilts that puffed about her.

"Nani," Meredith whispered, "are you awake?"

She seemed to nod a bit.

"It's after ten at night and Lucy's in bed. The dogs are fed and let out."

"Where's Sammy?" Nani whispered.

Meredith rubbed an ice chip over the old woman's chapped lips. "He's gone to make tea. He's staying on awhile, Nani."

"Good."

The room was filled with the work of Nani's hands—painted

knickknacks, embroidered throw pillows, tie-dyed curtains, a knotted rag rug, and Lucy's nearly finished quilt lying on a wooden chest under the window. A white wooden cross hung on a wall where Nani could see it from her bed, and Lucy's pictures surrounded the cross.

Meredith looked out to the night sky. The evening star, Venus they said, blinked low on the horizon. It had stormed again since Henry's drowning, the sun had risen and set as usual, the palms had waved in the trade winds. The birds gathered in the trees at dawn and dusk, singing as though nothing had changed.

But Eli and Alabar mooned about the house. They sniffed and whined at the closed study door.

"Nani, I don't know what to do," Meredith said as she returned to the bed. *"Henry's gone."*

The truth flooded her again and again, the suddenness of it, the surprise, the terrible truth and outrageous irony. For she knew how wrong she had been and how foolish.

Had she been in love with Henry Tennyson Fitzhugh? Was this what love felt like? She groaned, anguish twisting her heart. How cruel she had been. How arrogant. No one had ever loved her like Henry.

"You take care of Lucy?" Nani whispered, her eyes flickering.

"I will." Could she do that? Was her word worth anything?

"Promise," Nani said. "You stay here and take care of Lucy? Here, at Hana-lani?"

"I promise." Her tears tasted salty, and she raised a finger to her cheek to wipe them away.

"Call Kaelani & Tagami in Kahului. They drafted the will. They are kin. Hana-lani is Lucy's, from Mama. You will be trustee with Sammy. That way the others won't fight. Bring everyone here. Call today. *Do it.*"

"Yes, Nani." Sammy would know what she was talking about.

Meredith sat on the side of the bed and laid her head on Nani's chest. The woman's heartbeat was slow. A weak hand patted her hair.

"You loved Henry, after all, didn't you, Princess?" Nani whispered. "You didn't know."

"Yes."

"And you love Lucy too, don't you? She loves you back."

156

"Yes."

"You be okay, Princess, you be okay. You need to pray, you need to believe. You do your best, try your hardest, and you'll be okay. Lucy will teach you."

With those words, Meredith wept, wrapping her arms around Nani as though she were a life raft.

Twenty-three

The days merged together as though time stood still. The Sunday after Henry's drowning, Meredith phoned Parker. Lucy was coloring in the dining room, Nani had finished her breakfast tray and was sleeping, and Sam had gone to church.

"Parker, are you there?"

"Sorry, had another call come in. You said you don't know when you're coming home?"

"I'm staying on for a while."

"Why would you do that? Have you lost your mind?"

"You wouldn't understand." And she couldn't begin to explain. Nani would be leaving soon, she was sure. She slept too much, way too much. What would she do without Nani?

"Try me."

"I have some things to take care of." *Permanent things,* she thought.

"Well, keep me posted. Gotta go, kid."

"Parker..."

"Yeah?"

"Any news from...my father?"

"Looks like more bills."

"Could you open them?"

"Just a sec."

Meredith picked a cuticle as she waited. Her nails were short now, unpolished, but a natural luster was shining through the half moons.

"Here," Parker said. Paper rustled. "Looks to be second and third notices. And here...a note.... They're moving him June first to a welfare home."

Meredith swallowed hard. "Thanks, Parker." Was that Nick's voice in the background? Somehow, she didn't care.

"Meredith, do you need help?"

"I'm okay."

"Maybe I should fly out and rescue you."

"No need. I'll be home in a few weeks." *For one reason or another,* she thought, as her brain clouded with indecision. How could she move to Hana? Even if she did, she'd have to go back to the city to pack her things and settle her affairs. Her head was beginning to throb.

"You haven't asked about Nick."

"Right. Any news?"

"Meredith, there's something you should know."

"I think I already know. Nick is with *you*, right? You're *together?*"

"Yeah, I'm really sorry, like it just kind of happened. Never expected it. Believe me, I didn't plan it."

Meredith smiled. "I know. It's all right, Parker."

"I hope so. Listen, I gotta go. I'll call in a few days to make sure you're okay. You sound different. You worry me. You don't sound like the old Meredith."

"I'm fine. Call in a few days."

Meredith set the earpiece carefully on the black wall mount and turned toward Henry's study. It was time.

She opened the door, entered the airless room, and unlatched a window. She surveyed the desk, piled with his papers. Books were stacked on an ottoman and side table. She sat in his desk chair. It smelled of rum and spicy tobacco and...Henry. She ran her hand over the wooden arms and sighed. The scent of jasmine drifted in from the garden outside.

She reached for the picture of Maria. *A pretty girl,* Meredith thought. *A thoughtful girl.* She sensed too that Maria had been strong, determined, even aggressive. Was she the leader and Henry the follower? Probably. She slipped the framed photo into a drawer alongside a child's biography of Father Damien. She turned to the papers on the desk.

An outline listed categories with notes under each heading. Next to the outline was a copy of *Four Quartets*, a few pages turned down at the corners. She picked up the slim volume and opened to a highlighted passage:

But to apprehend
The point of intersection of the timeless
With time, is an occupation for the saint—
No occupation either, but something given
And taken, in a lifetime's death in love,
Ardour and selflessness and self-surrender.

Henry.

She studied the words, wrestling with them. Could she make sense of this? Could she assemble these papers and continue his work or find people who could? Could something good come from the mess she had made? She looked at his last notes. He had written in red ink and underlined the words, *Only the trying*. That was what he had said to her once, one could only try. Try what?

"Hi." Sammy stood in the open doorway, his hands in his pockets.

He wore chinos and a yellow polo shirt. He gave Meredith the impression of being complete, the way he held himself erect and purposeful, a short man made tall by his bearing. He pushed his Oakland A's cap back, wiped his brow with a measured stroke, and reset the cap neatly.

Meredith looked up. "Hi. How was church?"

"Nice. Haven't been in ages, but it seemed time. Thought it might help with Henry."

"Did it?"

"I think so. I might go again. It's not Nani's church, but it's my mama's and I grew up in it."

"Not Nani's? You went to the Catholic one? Are you Catholic?"

"Born and raised, but lapsed for some time." He looked at the papers on the desk. "You okay?"

"I suppose. Come in, Sammy, and keep me company. I think I'm still in shock."

Sammy's eyes were sad. "Me too. You know Henry invited me to go jogging with him? We never had the chance." He walked to the cedar chest and raised the lid. "I wondered if you'd seen his albums."

"Albums?"

"He has some good pictures."

"With Maria?"

"And here, at Hana-lani." He lifted out a thick binder.

Meredith breathed deeply, expecting to enter a world of both joy and pain. She feared that to know more of Henry would be to love more, and...to suffer more. Was love worth it?

"Maybe not, Sammy. Maybe another time."

But he had set it in front of her and was flipping the thick pages. Here was Henry as a boy with a little dark girl at his side, here he was fishing, here was a family picture in front of the church.

"There must be over fifty people here," Meredith said as she touched the black and white print.

"Yeah," he said, sighing. "Most of Hana is related."

"Do you think they'll find him?"

"It doesn't look good, Meredith."

"Don't say that."

"You know I loved him too." He turned to the window and looked out over the lawns.

"I know."

"I worshiped him. Ever since his class at Berkeley. He was brilliant. He changed my life, or at least his class did."

"How so?" How could a class change someone's life?

"I began to understand why things were the way they were, why we make the assumptions we make today. It's because of the past, all that has gone before us that influences our thoughts. The past doesn't always create our ideas, but it powerfully influences them."

"You sound like him." Meredith looked at Sammy's silhouette against the window.

"I suppose I do. I swallowed his words and have thought of them many times since."

She closed the album and stared at the leather cover.

Sammy shifted his weight and rubbed his hands as he turned to face her. "Meredith, I need to get back to Kahului tomorrow. I'll keep in touch by phone in the next few days to make sure you're okay, and Nani and Lucy too."

"I'd appreciate that."

"Want some lunch?"

"Sure."

"I'll find Lucy. Shall we eat on the verandah? I like being outside when I can." He turned in the doorway. "And Meredith...you should be able to take those bandages off now."

"I know," she said as she felt them with her fingertips. "But it's pretty ugly underneath."

"I understand. Keep them on as long as you like. I'll call you when lunch is ready."

"Thanks, Sammy."

⌘ ⌘ ⌘

That night, as Sammy read to Lucy in her room, Meredith walked to the library windows. She reached for the rods and opened the heavy draperies, pulling the rings over the thick pole. Through the wide-open window, the night sky was lit with the pale glow of a full moon, and the light bathed the walls of books. She listened to the surf crash below, far beyond the lawns, pulled by the moon. The breeze was warm, the night unconcerned with the cataclysmic events of her life, not caring whether she lived or died. The ocean would roll on forever, regardless.

Were these permanent things? Was she not? Was Henry not? Was he watching from a star to see if she would stay or go? Nani believed in an afterlife. Why couldn't she, Meredith? Could she try? She wanted to.

Wearily, Meredith climbed the stairs to bed, wondering what the library would look like with the sun streaming through the windows. Wouldn't Lucy be surprised!

She walked to the bath and looked in the mirror. She peeled the bandages off and examined her wounds. A long purple line extended from her forehead to her cheek. The skin was puffy and pale pink, like a newborn. She touched the area gently. Seemed okay. She tossed the bandages into the trash and smoothed on some of Nani's kukui oil. Her face wasn't perfect, but she didn't mind. She was, in an odd way, grateful for the crash, even the cuts, for they had brought her to Hana-lani.

Lucy's watercolor lay on her dresser. Stick-figure Henry stared through his wire-rims with his black-dot eyes. She ran her finger over the paint. He was a good man. Didn't goodness count? Wasn't that a permanent thing? If not, what was it? She found the most recent book he had given her and crawled into bed, *their* bed. She opened it to where she had left off, as though it held the key to his life, and possibly to hers.

It was Sunday, March 28, nearly five weeks since the crash.

⌘⌘⌘

Eli licked her arm as the morning light filtered through the curtains. How long had she slept? Lucy, still in her pajamas, sucked her thumb and gazed at her. Nani! How could she forget Nani?

She bolted out of bed and ran to the old woman's room. Tutu slept soundly, the quilt pulled up to her chin. Her breathing seemed regular.

Meredith dressed quickly. She fed the dogs and set out Lucy's cereal and milk as the water boiled for tea. *Henry.* Would these waves of sadness never end?

Sammy peeked into the kitchen. "Meredith? I'm leaving after I check once more on Nani."

"Okay. You'll come back?"

"Do you want me to?"

Meredith hesitated. "I do. I need you, Sammy. You'll take care of the lawyers like Nani wants?"

He breathed in deeply. "I'll have my uncle look at the will, and we'll have a meeting of the clan. But Nani may live through this after all. Let's not rush to judgment."

Meredith caught the hope in his voice and held on to it. "You think she'll be okay?"

"She has before."

"Maybe so. That would be wonderful." A weight lifted from Meredith's heart.

"Even so, we should review the will, to give her peace of mind, now that Henry...well...at the very least, we need a new trustee." His voice was thin.

Meredith approached his sturdy figure. She kissed him on the cheek and hugged him. He held her close. He smelled lemony.

"I'll be back," he said, pulling away. He smiled and gave a short salute. "Is Lucy going to be baptized soon? My aunt was asking."

"I don't know."

"It was supposed to happen at Easter."

"It's on the calendar." *How nosy she had been that day, how bored, how restless.*

"It would be good for Lucy."

"You believe in these things?"

"I don't know. I'm trying to keep an open mind. The jury's still out, as they say. I *want* to believe. Wouldn't it be something if it were all true? Like some fairy tale turning out to be real?"

"I don't know either." Would she ever know such things? "Want some breakfast? A little juice or coffee? Tea?"

"I'll pick up something on the way to town." He kissed her on the forehead, gave a little wave, and turned toward the entry.

"Thanks, Sammy."

"See you in a couple of days." He left to check on Nani.

⌘ ⌘ ⌘

Lucy cleared her dishes and grabbed Meredith's hand. "Reading time, Princess, reading time. When is Papa coming home?"

Meredith didn't reply. They walked into the library.

"The windows! The windows!" Lucy cried. "You opened the draperies!"

Meredith grinned and followed her across the room, absorbing the child's happiness.

Lucy placed her hands flat against the panes and stared out. The morning was like many at Hana-lani. Dark clouds hovered low over the sea. The sun would appear late, if at all.

"We'd better stay inside, I think." Meredith moved the rocker to the windows. "What shall we read today?"

Lucy handed her the *Book of Virtues* and squeezed into the chair, curling into Meredith's side. "The one about the wolf."

"The Boy Who Cried Wolf." She turned to the page. Sheep frolicked on a green hillside; a boy shouted to villagers.

Lucy pointed to the first word. "B-o-y," she sounded out.

"Excellent. Try this one." She pointed to *wolf.*

"W-o-l-f," she cried. "Cool. I did it."

"You sure did."

"Now *you* read the rest."

And Meredith read about the boy who had lied about a wolf threatening his sheep so many times that he was not believed when the real wolf appeared.

"Papa likes that one."

"Lucy, Papa has gone away...to be with Mama."

"I know."

"Papa loves you very much."

"I know." She looked up at Meredith. "And I'll be with them one day. They are in heaven. Nani will go there too and me too. We will all be together then."

Meredith tried to smile, but her lower lip refused, quivering.

"Don't cry, Miss Meredith, don't cry," Lucy said as she wiped Meredith's cheek with her fingers. "It will be all right."

Lucy jumped out of the rocker and pulled Meredith to the windows. They gazed over the fields to the sea as the sun broke through the clouds, shining a path on the waters.

And then Lucy began to dance.

Meredith watched her move, her toes tapping, her fingers weaving, her figure silhouetted against the land, sea, and sky. She thought of Henry, of his sacrifice, his life given for his daughter's, for love. She thought of Nick and felt only an odd numbness, as though something had been erased, something rotten had been cut out. She recalled her old longings, her emptiness and her fear, and found them curiously absent. Instead, she looked forward to these moments with the little girl, the conversations with the old woman, and petting the dogs. She looked forward to Sammy looking in on them. She even looked forward to Easter and Lucy's baptism. Maybe she could learn to sew. She could finish the quilt.

Sammy would help her do what needs to be done. Maybe he could work on Maria's manuscript, contact the publisher Henry mentioned. Maybe he could tell her more about Henry, his parents, what he was like.... Maybe he could be a friend and help with Lucy.

Lucy paused, and turned, beckoning to Meredith to dance with her.

Meredith shook her head. She returned to the rocker and her reverie as the child danced, her fingers pointing and waving, her toes tapping.

Meredith would speak to Nani about letting Hana School use the house and grounds. And about the Debate Club meetings. She could work with the family at the meeting. Would they listen to her? With Sammy there to help? There was so much to do, raising Lucy. Some day she'd take her to her to Caulfield College and show her around. And to New York and Paris. Why, she'd be Lucy's Aunt Julia.

She needed an income. She didn't feel right living off the child. She'd start a business here in Hana. Maybe an art gallery? She'd call the university in Honolulu and see if they might like to participate. She envisioned guest speakers and fundraisers for the Senior Center. She could teach art classes.

Her father would like to see this, she thought, as she gazed over the fields. She would call Florida in the morning, and after that, the airlines. Her father would like Hana-lani, she was sure of it.

Lucy held out her hand again, and this time Meredith took it, following her in the dance before the morning sun, one step at a time.

Epilogue

Easter morning, people poured out the front doors of the Congregational Church, chatting and hugging and shaking hands.

Meredith slipped behind the wheel of the VW van parked nearby and checked Lucy's seatbelt. The child looked so big sitting there in the front passenger seat with her white dress and little veil. Surely her brown legs had grown another two inches in the last week. Meredith looked back at Sammy and Nani sitting behind them and smiled.

"We did it," Nani said. "Lucy's baptized. Praise Jesus!" The finished quilt lay folded neatly on her lap.

"Praise Jesus!" Lucy cried and clapped her hands.

Sammy chuckled.

"I wish Henry was here," Nani said quietly, as though speaking to herself.

Meredith inserted the key into the ignition. The engine turned over several times, threatening to flood, and finally caught.

"Me too," Sammy said.

Meredith kept her eyes on the highway as they wound north along the coast to Hana-lani. The week before, Henry's memorial service had been well attended. Pastor Kanuki's words were thoughtful and soothing about Henry's good life and how he was in heaven with his folks, the great missionaries in Indonesia, and now with Maria too. The head of Henry's department at UC Berkeley had flown out and said some nice things about his accomplishments and his fine mind. Several cousins played ukuleles while everyone sang. An uncle spoke about Henry's spirit joining the universe and another cousin talked about Henry coming back to earth as a better man as he climbed the ladder of life, and Nani had shaken her head, mumbling, *the old way, the old way, tsk tsk*. Lucy read a poem and some folks cried.

They hadn't found Henry's body so there wasn't a burial, and for some reason that made Meredith especially sad.

Now, as they wound up the highway, she thought of Henry and a terrible longing gripped her. It was a visceral pull, tearing her heart.

Turning up the gravel drive, she noted Parker hadn't moved her rental to the side. Nick's surfboard remained where he had left it on the front lawn, sinking in, making a rut. The two of them had been at Hana-lani three days, and Meredith was fed up.

She helped Lucy out of the van and Sammy helped Nani. Lucy ran ahead through the house to the back verandah and down to the lawn, the dogs yapping at her heals in joy.

"Miss Parker! Miss Parker!" she cried. "I'm baptized! I'm baptized! The pastor poured water on my head!"

Meredith followed.

Nick, wearing a nylon jockey, was sprawled on a chaise in the sun. He stared intently into a tiny screen as he punched a keypad. Parker lay on a chaise next to him, catching the rays as well. A wire connected her earphones to a portable CD player, and she tapped pink nails on the machine's chrome surface. Her orange bikini was covered with gold sparkles running in concentric circles. Meredith had forgotten how large her bust was. Her freckled breasts spilled out of the thin fabric, as though desperately trying to breathe.

Lucy danced around the sunbathers, clapping her hands and flouncing her white dress. She had kicked her shoes off, black patents Meredith had ordered from a Honolulu catalog, and Meredith wondered where her veil had landed. Eli sniffed Parker's toes and Parker waved him off as she muttered under her breath. Alabar paced.

Meredith handed Parker a tube of sunscreen. "Be careful, kid, you're fair. This sun is a killer."

Parker waved it away. "How was church?"

"Fine."

Nick gazed up at her. "Hi there," he said. He grinned appreciatively as he scanned her body, an inspection that once made her tremble. "Looking good, Meredith." He sipped from his beer. "Sweet color on you." He *was* well built—strong calves, tight abdomen, muscular chest and biceps. She recalled once nibbling his chest hairs. *Yuk.*

"Thanks." Meredith wore the coral sheath and Lucy's shell lei. She had used extra makeup on the long scars. "Can I get you guys anything?" She tried to sound sarcastic, but they didn't catch it.

"Nah, we're good." Nick lay back and closed his eyes. "This is a great place you have here, Mer."

"I can see why you didn't want to leave right away," Parker said into the sky as she moistened her lips with her tongue.

Meredith sat down on the edge of Nick's lounge. "I think it's time, Nick." She looked at Parker. "You too, Parker."

Parker rose on an elbow and lowered her dark glasses. She wore gold hoop earrings that flashed in the sun, and her breasts nearly made their escape as she leaned forward.

"Time?" the two of them chorused.

"*To go.*" Meredith stood and headed for the house. She turned. "Pack your things. You're taking the morning flight. To Kahului at least. From there it's up to you."

"What?" they said.

Parker scowled. "Come on, Meredith, what's the problem?"

"We just got here." Nick offered his most charming, most adorable look. His blue eyes grew wide and his perfect brows rose a fraction. He inclined slightly forward, palms open. He grinned, showing his straight, bleached teeth.

Meredith eyed the two of them. "Tough break. We're not running a hotel. Lucy, come on in. It's time for lunch." She wondered if Sammy had remembered to hide the dyed eggs in the front garden. Wouldn't Lucy be surprised!

Only the trying, Meredith thought as she followed the little bare feet and the white cotton flounces and the brown curls up the verandah stairs. She could do that. She could *try.*

That's all Henry would have asked. And oddly enough, *before* the moment she tried to do the right thing, it seemed like sacrifice, but *after* it didn't seem like sacrifice at all. It just felt good. She would ask Sammy about that. Or maybe Nani. It was curious, curious but nice.

Only the trying. Meredith took Lucy's hand and headed for the kitchen.

OFFERINGS

Christine Sunderland

Jack's haunted by fears of the past.
Madeleine holds a powerful secret.
And Rachelle is running away.

For the last seventeen years, her husband, Jack, and son, Justin, have
been Madeleine Seymour's world. Then, during Justin's wedding
reception, Jack collapses. Jack needs surgery, and he insists it be
performed by the doctor who perfected the procedure. But the doctor
isn't reachable, and time is running out.

Dr. Rachelle DuPres, plagued by memories of a deadly failure, flees
America to search out her roots in her ancestral village in Provence,
France. But as she tries to locate the graves of her Catholic uncles and
her Jewish parents, will their roles in the Holocaust bring more angst—or
the answers she so desperately seeks?

A poignant story about choices made along the way...
and the miracles of the heart.
Set in the breathtaking beauty of France.

www.ChristineSunderland.com
MyTravels.ChristineSunderland.com
www.oaktara.com

INHERITANCE

Christine Sunderland

She risked everything to save a life...
But who would save hers?

Vietnamese-American Victoria Nguyen, seventeen, flees to England with a powerful secret...and a determined senator on her trail.

Madeleine Seymour, a history professor, and her husband, Jack, a retired wine broker, travel from San Francisco to London to purchase property for a children's home—and find much more than land at stake.

Brother Cristoforo, a black Franciscan from the Seymours' Quattro Coronati orphanage in Rome, wrestles with demons of his past and present.

Woven through the mists of Lent to new life on Easter Day, *Inheritance* draws the lives of these four characters together to a stunning, unforgettable conclusion.

A poignant story about choices made along the way...
and the miracles of the heart.
Set in the breathtaking beauty of England.

www.ChristineSunderland.com
MyTravels.ChristineSunderland.com
www.oaktara.com

About the Author

CHRISTINE SUNDERLAND, author of the trilogy, *Pilgrimage, Offerings,* and *Inheritance,* has long been interested in the formation of cultural ideals in American society, and the role of  history and tradition in the public square. In her visits to Hawaii she has appreciated the respect for faith and family she has found there, as well as the stunning natural world, both beautiful and dangerous.

She is currently Church Schools Director for the Anglican Province of Christ the King and Vice-President of the American Church Union (*Anglicanpck.org*). She has edited *The American Church Union Church School Series, The Anglican Confirmation Manual,* and *Summer Lessons.* She has authored *Teaching the Church's Children* and seven children's novellas, the *Jeanette Series,* published by the American Church Union.

Christine holds a B.A. in English Literature *cum laude.* She is an alumna of the Squaw Valley Writers Workshop and the Maui Writers Retreat.

www.ChristineSunderland.com
MyTravels.ChristineSunderland.com
www.oaktara.com

CPSIA information can be obtained at www.ICGtesting.com
Printed in the USA
LVOW090524210612

287052LV00002B/152/P